GW01186151

ISBN 0 9535873 0 4

behind closed doors

the hidden structure within the Orange camp [the Royal Arch Purple Order] examined from an evangelical perspective.

by W.P. Malcomson

Published by:

Evangelical Truth
PO Box 69
Banbridge
BT32 4RS

All Scriptural quotations are taken from the Authorized King James Version of the Holy Bible

All proceeds from this book will go directly to Christian Outreach.

contents

dedication

Dedicated to my late father Will Malcomson who brought me up in the fear and admonition of God. And having faithfully preached the Word of God for many years taught me by example that I was saved to serve.

acknowledgements

My most humble thanks to all those who have helped and encouraged me in the preparation of this book. For all those who have assisted me in the furtherance of the message whether in meetings or in one to one encounters. For all those who have practically and unselfishly assisted me in researching, proofing, publishing and distributing the book, whether inside or outside the Loyal Orders. For all those who have faithfully prayed for me through the good and the bad times. To God be the glory.

preface

Whilst most people today are aware of the existence of the Loyal Orange Institution and the Royal Black Institution, few have heard *anything* about the existence of a highly secretive institution that is sandwiched between the aforementioned bodies - the **Royal Arch Purple Order**. This institution, which has tens of thousands of members in Ireland, in Britain, and throughout the British Commonwealth, has succeeded, where other secret societies have failed, in concealing its secrets and mysteries from outside scrutiny.

The purpose of this research has been to break through the veil of mystery and secrecy surrounding the Royal Arch Purple Order and to examine it from an evangelical perspective. In doing so we are primarily directing this publication at fellow believers, especially those within the Royal Arch Purple, enabling fair, open and informed analysis of the subject. The Lord Jesus Christ said, "**For there is nothing hid, which shall not be manifested; neither was any thing kept secret, but that it should come abroad**" (Mark 4:22).

In addressing such a sensitive matter we are aware that some may question our actions or even misunderstand our motives, but it is our simple desire to lift up the name of our beloved Saviour the Lord Jesus Christ and to "**earnestly contend for the faith**" (Jude v3).

We take the Word of God as our guide in this endeavour, believing it to be the inerrant, infallible, fully inspired Word of Truth. We look upon the Scriptures alone as the unadulterated source of our argument and say in the words of evangelical author Vance Havner, "The Word of God is either absolute or obsolete." We look upon this precious book, as the final authority on all matters of faith and practice. As Jesus said, "**Man shall not live by bread alone, but by every word that proceedeth out of the mouth of God**" (Matthew 4:4).

In addressing this subject we are primarily trying to establish whether the origins, practices, teaching and symbolism of the Royal Arch Purple are compatible with the infallible truth of God's Word or whether, as some evangelicals claim, the Order is nothing better than veiled Freemasonry embodying much unbiblical error, and therefore worthy of condemnation.

The Royal Arch Purple Order has always portrayed itself as a bastion of the Protestant Faith, which is firmly committed to scriptural practices and principles. It is therefore our aim to examine the strength and validity of such claims in light of the material before us. The Bible declares: "**Prove all things; hold fast that which is good. Abstain from all appearance of evil**" (1Thessalonians 5:21-22).

This book is not an attack upon Protestantism nor is it designed to undermine the traditional Unionist/Loyalist position. We have no axe to grind with any individual within the Royal Arch Purple, nor is it our intention to embarrass anyone by the publication of this book.

Lorraine Boettner in his book 'Roman Catholicism' ably outlines the evangelical Protestant position on traditionalism when he affirms, "We do not reject all tradition, but rather make judicious use of it in so far as it accords with Scripture and is founded on truth." Any time there has been a measure of true reform within the Church, there is nothing held valid simply because of antiquity or tradition. Men have submitted themselves to the instruction of God's Word, abandoning the objectionable teachings and inventions of man.

God commands in His Word, "**What thing soever I command you, observe to do it: thou shalt not add thereto, nor diminish from it**" (Deuteronomy 12:32). We clearly see that no rite or practice other than that which is expressly commanded in Scripture, should be found among God's people. The great Charles H. Spurgeon puts it very succinctly, "The Bible, the whole Bible and nothing but the Bible."

It is our great hope that through reading this publication many people will come to a real understanding of the true character and workings of the Royal Arch Purple and that those believers within the Order will prayerfully consider the material outlined. Jesus said, "**when he, the Spirit of truth, is come, he will guide you into all truth**" (John 16:13).

introduction

Before examining the Royal Arch Purple Order and its initiation ceremony - the Royal Arch Purple degree, we must first establish its location within the Loyal Orders today. By doing such we must clear up any ambiguity or misunderstanding which remains on the subject both from within and outside the Order.

Contrary to popular belief, the Royal Arch Purple degree does NOT reside within the Loyal Orange Institution of *Ireland* although it does exist within the Orange Institution in nearly every other country throughout the British Commonwealth. The Orange Institution of Ireland, from the formation of its ruling Grand Lodge in 1798, only ever accepted two degrees, namely, that of Orange and Plain Purple, and has NEVER in its history owned the Royal Arch Purple degree. The Plain Purple lecture teaches every Orangeman that the Orange and Plain Purple are "the only two orders recognised by the Grand Orange Lodge of Ireland."

The Royal Arch Purple Chapter, a separate organisation formed in 1911, does however possess the Royal Arch Purple degree as its sole degree. Whilst the Orange Order has always, by its rules, dissociated itself from the Royal Arch Purple degree, the far smaller Independent Loyal Orange Institution employs the degree as an integral part of its Order. The layout of its degree system is outlined in the Independent Orange 'candidate instruction' booklet which states: "There are three degrees in the Institution, the first being the Orange...Upon receipt of the Plain Purple degree a member is entitled to hold office in his Private Lodge and to attend the meetings of District. The Royal Arch Purple degree is the longest and most detailed degree. A member who receives this degree can attend County and Imperial Grand Lodge meetings." This degree, worked within the Independent Orange, is in essence the same as that employed by the Royal Arch Purple Chapter, although like any distinct organisation it has some slight differences.

degree layout

Loyal Orange Institution. (2 degrees)
1st degree: Orange degree
2nd degree: Plain Purple degree

Independent Loyal Orange Institution (3 degrees)
1st degree: Orange degree
2nd degree: Plain Purple degree
3rd degree: Royal Arch Purple degree

Royal Arch Purple Chapter (1 degree)
Royal Arch Purple degree

Obtaining any useful information on the Royal Arch Purple degree is fraught with many difficulties due mainly to the fact that both the Royal Arch Purple Chapter and the Independent Orange Institution are secret societies which zealously guard their secrets and mysteries from the uninitiated. It is fair to say they have succeeded in guarding their practices, teaching and symbolism over the years where even Freemasonry has failed. Published material on the degree is therefore rare.

The only evangelical analysis, of any substance, examining the Royal Arch Purple that one can uncover, relates to a small, little known pamphlet published in 1925 by the "Protestant Truth Society" called 'Orangeman or Christian: Which?' It was written by former Deputy Grand Chaplain of the Grand Orange Lodge of England the Rev. Alexander Roger and was a *condemnation* of the Royal Arch Purple degree. It was a limited edition internal document, being circulated exclusively within the Orange family. This booklet was a final appeal from evangelicals within the Orange Order in England to purge the Royal Arch Purple degree out of the Orange Institution of England (after its introduction into the Order in 1913). This effort failed and resulted in many believers resigning from the Orange, including the writer of the pamphlet the Rev. Roger, minister of Immanuel Church, Putney. Editing the booklet was J.A. Kensit. He was the son of the founder of the Society who was killed by devout Roman Catholics because of his work for Protestantism. J.A. Kensit was not afforded the opportunity to resign, but was expelled by the Orange for his part in the publication.

The only other publication that we can find on the subject comes from within the Royal Arch Purple Chapter itself. Produced in late 1993, this book called 'History of the Royal Arch Purple Order', was also of limited circulation and was addressed primarily to its own membership. The references to the Arch Purple degree were understandably shrouded in veiled language. Such was in keeping with the rules of the Order which prevent the contents of the degree being written down anywhere, thus protecting the secrets and mysteries of the Order from being obtained by the uninitiated. The Royal Arch Purple Chapter justifies this position in their book by stating: "It is well to remind ourselves of the constraints, which are placed upon us. The Rev. John Brown in his short account of the foundations of the Royal Black Institution put it very succinctly, 'the things of the temple must be learned in the temple' " (p. 191).

When examining this general subject we were blessed to be supplied with a *draft* of the Royal Arch Purple book. This was a compilation that was more explicit in detail than the actual book. After studying the draft, it is evident that the passages relating to the initiation have been heavily amended in the published book. Clearly *somebody* was not happy at the frank comparisons between the Royal Arch Purple Order and the Masonic Order! We will, however, allude to this revealing draft where and when relevant, as it includes some helpful material to this research.

Some other books have made passing allusions to the Royal Arch Purple Order in the past, when covering other similar societies, although these references are scarce.

While we will employ all three aforementioned sources to assist us in our research we will principally examine the *actual text* of the Royal Arch Purple degree, which we have providentially received in full. Such material has never been publicly revealed or examined before. Even many Royal Arch Purple men are ignorant of the teaching of their Order as they can only obtain it through listening attentively to the lecturers during the prolonged Arch Purple initiation ceremony. Such texts are kept exclusively within the domain of the lecturing fraternity, and in keeping with all other secret societies it is ultimately maintained as an oral tradition. The Arch Purple lecturers, like all Royal Arch Purple men, are oath-bound never to write down the contents of the degree.

Whilst we are analysing the Royal Arch Purple Order on its own merits, using its own material and teaching for examination, we will explore any parallels between the Masonic Order and the Royal Arch Purple Order. Moreover we will relate any similarities that exist between the two bodies. When referring to Freemasonry in this book we mean speculative (or esoteric) Freemasonry, which was formed in 1717. While it is not the prime focus of this research, it is important to state that the broad evangelical fundamentalist body has always resolutely opposed the evil existence and encroachments of Freemasonry.

When we refer to the 'Royal Arch Purple Order', and to 'Royal Arch Purple men' in this book we are describing the entire membership of the Royal Arch Purple Chapter. We are also including all those within the Independent Orange Institution who have acquired this 'third degree' of their Order. In a wider context we are referring to every Orangeman throughout the world who has been initiated into the Arch Purple Order in their respective jurisdictions.

We will at times refer to the 'Royal Arch Purple Order' as the 'Royal Arch Purple' or the 'Arch Purple' for short, and to 'Royal Arch Purple men' as 'Arch Purple men', these terms meaning the same thing. We will also refer to 'Freemasonry' as 'Masonry' or the 'Masonic Order' and a 'Freemason' as a 'Mason', these terms being also the same.

chapter 1

the source of the degree

The Loyal Orange Institution was formed on 21st September 1795 shortly after the 'Battle of the Diamond' outside Loughgall, Co. Armagh. Three well-known local men of the area, James Wilson, Dan Winter, and James Sloan, established the institution. Whilst much is made of these 'founding fathers' within Orange circles; from a spiritual perspective we see no evidence that any of them had evangelical credentials. History, in fact, shows that all three men were dedicated Freemasons and two of the three were actually proprietors of licensed premises.

The Bible addresses such people, saying, "**Woe unto him that giveth his neighbour drink, that puttest thy bottle to him, and makest him drunken also, that thou mayest look on their nakedness!**" (Habakkuk 2:15). The Rev. Allan Dunlop, addressing this passage of Scripture in his book 'Where Shadows Fall' (p.37), says, "The curse of God is upon the drink trade for what profits it brings are wrung from widows tears, children's terror, women's virtue and young men's strength; and of wives and mothers broken hearts."

It is true to say that Dan Winter came from a Quaker background, although his ungodly lifestyle shows he was anything but a dedicated Quaker. Firstly, Quakers have always practised strict 'total abstinence' and have always opposed the devilish influence of alcohol. *Winter was the proprietor of a public house.* Secondly, Quakers have always been opposed to the heathenish practices and teachings of Freemasonry. *Winter was a zealous Freemason.* Thirdly, Quakers have always been pacifists, opposing all type of fighting. *Winter was the leader of the local 'Peep O' Day Boys'* (an illegal Protestant militia group of the day), *and he was also a well-known 'cock fighter' in the area.*

The 'Battle of the Diamond' itself lasted only fifteen minutes and was centred on Dan Winter's public house, which was located at the Diamond crossroads. This battle (or skirmish) resulted in Winter's premises being burnt to the ground by the attacking Roman Catholics who were ironically known as 'the Defenders'. This place was the special focus of the attack as it was the gathering house for the local 'Peep O' Day Boys'. Prior to the battle, the authorities had made several arrests and various arms seizures relating to this illegal group.

Winter's supporters, many of whom were Freemasons, gathered around the debris of the public house and pledged themselves to form a new secret society, made up wholly of Protestant men. Now that they no longer had Winter's premises as a meeting place the men retired to James Sloan's public house in the local village of Loughgall. Here the Orange Institution was properly organised.

The founders of the Orange Institution were known as 'unwarranted', 'clandestine' or 'hedge' Masons. These Masons were a rebellious group who would not accept the existing degree format of the ruling Masonic Grand Lodge of the day. Belinda Loftus, in her book 'Mirrors' (p.24), confirms that the clandestine or hedge Masons were "unwarranted by the Grand Lodge in Dublin" because Irish Masonry "refused to recognise any degrees but craft." Up until the early 1800s the Grand *Masonic* Lodge of Ireland only accepted three degrees, - Entered Apprentice, Fellowcraft and Master Mason, collectively known as the 'Craft degrees' or the 'Blue Lodge'. All other degrees were held to be illegal.

The Unwarranted Masons were the more zealous (or esoteric) Masons who adhered to the many mystical degrees, which today are accepted within the domain of *higher degree Freemasonry*. These degrees are found under the auspices of the Red Lodge, known as the Chapter and the Chivalry degrees, known as the Preceptory.

The Irish Masonic publication 'History of Freemasonry in the Province of

Antrim' alludes to these clandestine Masons. It explain how these men would ascend to "the top of some neighbouring hill, and there, towards the close of a summers evening, after the manner of the ancient Druids, perform their rites and ceremonies, the meeting being properly tyled and guarded...They were unwarranted and recognised no authority and no authority recognised them" (p.143&144).

Winter, Sloan and Wilson, accompanied by others, felt the great need to instigate a ceremony of initiation into the new body and not surprisingly Freemasonry was chosen as the model. Initially the Orange had one sole degree known simply as the 'Orange degree'. As the months progressed the founding fathers introduced a further degree somewhere around late 1796. The 'Orange Marksman' degree as it was originally designated, became better known as the 'Purple degree'. It was constructed in Portadown, in the home of prominent Freemason, John Templeton - a location frequently used for Masonic ceremonies. Orange historian (and well known Freemason of his day) Colonel R.H. Wallace outlined in his 'History of the Orange Order' (1899) how the founders "were observed going into and out of a house in which a Masonic Lodge held its meetings," and that, "He [Mr Templeton] invited them into the Masonic room, and there and then satisfactory arrangements were made." He concluded by saying, "*the influence of the place and its associations can be discerned in the results*" (p. 50). Another Orange historian R.M. Sibbett in 'Orangeism in Ireland and Throughout the Empire' (1938) explained how, "The subject uppermost in their minds was touched upon and discussed, and, at the request of Mr. Templeton, *they adjourned to a room which had been used for other ceremonies*. Here the warrant was produced, the lodge was reopened, and a higher Order was added."

A further degree was added as Orangeism consolidated itself. The Royal Arch Purple Chapter book states that, "Probably late in the year 1796 or early 1797 a third degree known as Purple Marksman was added to the ritual. It is likely to have been composed by the same hands, probably in the same room as that of the Orange Marksman or Purpleman" (History of the Royal Arch Purple Order p. 39).

Whilst little is known of the *exact* content of these three degrees it seems certain that they were highly ritualistic in character, being modelled on the first three degrees of Freemasonry, namely, Entered Apprentice, Fellowcraft and Master Mason. The Royal Arch Purple Chapter book testifies that these three initial Orange degrees were "elaborate degrees" (p. 59).

Orange degree → Entered Apprentice degree
Orange Marksman degree → Fellowcraft degree
Purple Marksman degree → Master Mason degree

These were the three main degrees that were worked within the Order between 1795 and 1798, although many other ritualistic degrees were finding their way into Orangeism throughout the island of Ireland. Most of these degrees can today be found within the Royal Black Institution.

During this early period each individual Orange lodge administered its own control over the working of degrees, as no controlling authority existed to govern the degree system. A Grand Lodge of Ulster, as it were, was formed on 12th of July 1797, although it seemed to exercise little power over the whole island of Ireland.

The prevailing confusion within the Order, coupled with a large influx of new members, due to the deteriorating political situation in the form of the Republican uprising of the 'United Irelanders', resulted in the formation of a Grand Orange Lodge of Ireland on 21st April 1798. This brought much needed stability and leadership to the Order at a strategic period in its history.

Grand Lodge immediately addressed the bewildering amount of unnecessary ritualism that had found its way into Orangeism, and here began a process of reform which purged out all the ritualistic baggage which had settled itself within the Order. This resulted in the disposal of the original three (elaborate) degrees of the Orange. These were replaced with two simplified degrees of 'Orange' and 'Plain Purple'. Out with the old degrees went the old leadership of James Wilson, Dan Winter, and James Sloan.

Wasting little time, Grand Lodge released a strong statement on 13th December 1798 which reflected the hierarchy's strong desire to separate themselves from former error, stating: "*That many persons having introduced various Orders into the Orange Society which will very much tend to injure the regularity of the institution. The Grand Lodge disavows any Order but Orange and Purple and there can be none other regular unless issuing and approved by them.*"

From this date forward, the Grand Orange Lodge of Ireland accepted only two degrees within the Order - 'Orange' and 'Plain Purple'. Between 1798 and 1800 Grand Lodge began a process of implementing this simplification by standardising procedures throughout every lodge in Ireland. That they might eradicate any lingering injurious behaviour by spurious characters, they abolished the old Orange Order in 1800, with its ritualistic connections, obliging every Orangeman to rejoin a now simplified new Orange Institution.

Those ritualistic Orangemen inside the Order who bore allegiance to the former neo-Masonic degrees were far from happy at this radical reform. Some continued to practise these illegal degrees in a clandestine manner, in blatant violation of the rules of the Grand Orange Lodge of Ireland.

Facing strong persecution from a now powerful Grand Lodge and realising their beleaguered position, they merged the three old degrees into one large ritualistic degree. The Arch Purple Chapter's book 'History of the Royal Arch Purple Order' explains: "Sometime between 1800 and 1811, possibly in 1802, a new degree was devised by the Brethren who valued and loved the old traditions and who were concerned by the turn of events" (p. 58). This degree was "developed from the three pre 1798 'old degrees' " (p. 59). ***This elaborate degree became known as the 'Royal Arch Purple degree'***.

Three old degrees		Merged into
Orange degree Orange Marksman degree Purple Marksman degree	}	Royal Arch Purple degree

The Arch Purple Chapter's book also confirms its composition, how that it was designed to "include as much as possible of the travel and ritual of the original three." The draft to the Arch Purple Chapter's book diplomatically traces the roots of the Royal Arch Purple degree, stating that, "In light of the evidence available it would appear that the degree given today evolved from certain practices which had their origin in the Masonic Order, together with some innovations which had been introduced by those brethren conferring the degree in different areas being added to the original theme of the pre 1800 degrees to form a new ritual." Even this guarded statement was omitted from the published book!

Nevertheless, in their book 'The Orange Order: An Evangelical Perspective' Grand Chaplain of the Grand Orange Lodge of Scotland (which owns the Royal Arch Purple as its third degree) Rev. Ian Meredith and Irish Arch Purple man Rev. Brian Kennaway comment on the Arch Purple degree. They state, "It has to be admitted that this is the most 'Masonic-like' part of our ceremony." They later describe it as "***a Christianised or 'Reformed Freemasonry'***" (pp. 12, 25).

From its inception, the Grand Orange Lodge of Ireland looked upon this neo-Masonic Royal Arch Purple degree with understandable abhorrence. It was viewed as being incompatible with, and contrary to, both Protestantism and Orangeism. Those ritualistic Orangemen who practised the degree were persecuted by Grand Lodge, forcing them to practise the degree in great secrecy for fear of expulsion from the Order. Grand Lodge maintained this position throughout the whole of the 1800s and into the early 20th century. The hard line assumed by the Orange Institution in Ireland mirrored the resolute stance of Orangeism throughout Great Britain.

By the start of the 1900s many of these rebellious Orangemen throughout the British Isles had subtly worked themselves into positions of responsibility within their respective Grand Lodges. This provided them with ideal opportunities to pursue their covert aims.

In 1902 the Grand Orange Lodge of Scotland capitulated and accepted the Royal Arch Purple degree as an *integral part* of its Institution. This was achieved by replacing the Plain Purple degree with the Royal Arch Purple degree, thus maintaining a two-degree system.

The success of these ritualistic Orangemen in Scotland encouraged their Irish counterparts to bring a proposal to the Grand Orange Lodge of Ireland to accept the Royal Arch Purple degree into their Institution. In their endeavours they succeeded in that it passed two readings, but when it came before the Grand Lodge meeting of 8th December 1909, in Dublin, delegates present resolutely rejected the introduction of the Royal Arch Purple degree into the Orange Institution of Ireland.

Realising there was little chance of the Arch Purple degree being integrated into the Orange Institution of Ireland, these clandestine Orangemen, on 30th November 1911, inaugurated their own Institution - the "Royal Arch Purple Chapter of Ireland"- with its own ruling authority known as the Grand Chapter. The formation of the Grand Chapter seemed to give the Arch Purple a respectability they never before enjoyed, albeit it was still looked upon with suspicion by most within the Orange Institution in Ireland.

This significant event inspired those ritualistic Orangemen in England who adhered to the Royal Arch Purple degree to increase pressure upon their Grand Lodge for acceptance of the degree. Their subtle campaign finally succeeded, for in 1913 the Grand Orange Lodge of England accepted the Royal Arch Purple degree as an *integral part* of its Institution. This was achieved by adding the Royal Arch Purple degree to the two existing degrees, thus making it the third degree. This alteration proved to be Orangeism's final one to date. The Orange degree system remaining as follows:

Loyal Orange Institution of **Ireland**. (2 degrees)
1st degree: Orange degree
2nd degree: Plain Purple degree

Loyal Orange Institution of **Scotland**. (2 degrees)
1st degree: Orange degree
2nd degree: Royal Arch Purple degree

Loyal Orange Institution of **England**. (3 degrees)
1st degree: Orange degree
2nd degree: Plain Purple degree
3rd degree: Royal Arch Purple degree

Whilst the mistrust towards the Royal Arch Purple degree in Ireland prevailed for many years, the Arch Purple Grand Chapter, at its formation in 1911, introduced subtle procedures which over time would create the psychological image that the Arch Purple degree was a progressive step within the Orange Order. They deemed that one could not obtain the Arch Purple degree unless in good standing within the Orange Institution. They also held that any local Orange Lodge which formed its own private Royal Arch Purple Chapter, was expected to use the same lodge number for the Arch Purple as they did in the Orange (e.g. LOL 100, RAPC 100), thus deceptively blurring the differences between the two Orders. These policies were installed behind Orange backs.

As the 20th century has progressed most Orange Lodges simply hold their Royal Arch Purple meeting at the end of an Orange meeting. This occurs (normally) once a quarter. The Lodge is 'closed' and then reopened as a Royal Arch Purple Chapter. This is called 'raising the meeting'. All Orangemen, who are not yet Arch Purple men, are required to leave. This practice again portrays an image, in the minds of the uninformed, that the Arch Purple degree is a higher degree within the Orange Institution.

The Royal Arch Purple Chapter, also, arrogantly appropriated the 'Royal' prefix to their newly formed Institution without any prior authorisation. This self-conferment reinforced the rogue nature of the Arch Purple Order as the Crown alone is the only lawful authority that can perform the granting of such an important title. Such conferment can only be bestowed as a sign of royal recognition. The criteria for using the 'Royal' prefix is outlined in 'The Royal Encyclopaedia', which states: "Permission to use the title 'Royal' in front of the name of an institution or body... has long been a mark of royal favour. These honours, which are sparingly granted, are valued marks of royal recognition... the grant of the title 'Royal' is a matter of royal prerogative."

Today, the Royal Arch Purple Chapter still flaunts this 'Royal' title, as if, somehow, they are the focus of royal favour. The 'Royal' prefix also gives the Institution a respectability it has never hitherto earned. Moreover the Chapter can never argue that such a title refers to the scriptural 'royal priesthood' as such a description pertains solely to God's elect. It seems that the title relates more to the Order's links with Freemasonry, which promotes its members from the Blue Lodge or Craft Masonry (the first three degrees) to the Red Lodge where the Mason is initiated into the 'Royal Arch degree'.

As the years have passed by, the former hostility from the Grand Orange Lodge of Ireland towards the Royal Arch Purple degree has all but been extinguished. The Arch Purple Chapter has exploited the 20th Century indifference, existing within Grand Lodge, by portraying the Arch Purple degree as a natural step of advancement within the Orange Institution. This practice has prevailed, despite the Arch Purple Order still being debarred by Orangeism's own rules. The second degree of the Orange Order *still* outlines in its question and answer catechism:

Q. ***"Have you a number?***
A. ***Yes.***
Q. ***What is your number?***
A. ***One and another one which makes my number 2.***
Q. ***What 2?***
A. ***The Orange and Purple the only two orders recognised by the Grand Orange Lodge of Ireland " (Purple hear meaning Plain Purple).***

A potential candidate to the Royal Arch Purple cannot come of his own accord; he must first be chosen by the Order and then discreetly asked by those within.

Every member of the Royal Black Institution must first pass through the Royal Arch Purple Chapter before advancing into the Black Institution. All members of the Royal Black Institution have completed this elaborate degree.

Little is disclosed of the actual numerical strength of the Royal Arch Purple Chapter's membership. Estimates of the size of the Orange Institution of Ireland (from which the Arch Purple recruits) vary between 40,000 and 100,000 members. Informed sources within the hierarchy of the Chapter estimate that 95% of Orangemen today join the Royal Arch Purple Chapter and have therefore been initiated into this degree. Those within the Independent Loyal Orange Institution (which also employs the degree) believe their membership to be less than 1,500 members. So when calculating the influence of this degree in our Province today we see anything up to 95,000 men are subject to the Royal Arch Purple's oaths, rules and teaching. This figure is colossal (even if many of these men are lapsed or inactive members) when one thinks that you must be a *Protestant male over the age of 19* to join the Arch Purple Order. Allowing for this fact and the fact that there are only 500,000 Protestant males who live in Northern Ireland, up to one in three Protestant males (over the age of 19) could be under the influence of this neo-Masonic structure (including thousands of professing believers). This is amazing when coupled with an estimated 45,000 Craft Masons (first three degree Masons) in Northern Ireland, the overwhelming majority of which are Protestant males. Combining the strength of both institutions together totals *well over* 100,000 Protestant men.

There are also many more tens of thousands of Orangemen throughout the United Kingdom and the British Commonwealth who have also been initiated into this Order.

chapter 2

the binding of the candidate

Before being fully accepted as a Royal Arch Purple man the candidate must endure an elaborate initiation ceremony. This occurs on a night that is both mutually convenient to the candidate and the Chapter. Two District Lecturers are required to put the candidate through the initiation.

At the commencement of the ceremony the candidate is required to take a binding oath upon himself known within secret societies as an obligation (this is normally performed in a side room). In this oath he commits himself to the Royal Arch Purple Order, its secrets, mysteries and members.

Before the initiation, the candidate is asked to agree to participate in a ceremony he, as yet, knows nothing about. He is asked, "Do you now wish to receive the Royal Arch Purple degree?" Upon his positive affirmation the obligation is then introduced to him as follows: "Before we can impart to you any of the secrets or mysteries of the Royal Arch Purple degree you will be required to take upon yourself a solemn, sincere, *binding*, yet entirely voluntary obligation, *binding you to us, as we are bound to one another as Royal Arch Purple men.*" Here the lecturers surround the introduction to the oath in ambiguous language, albeit the child of God receives due notice, at this early stage, of the binding effect of the obligation.

The nature of the obligation is then deceptively described to the candidate, in the following terms. “There is nothing in that obligation that may prove detrimental to you in life, or hinder you in the duty you owe to God, your country, or yourself. Are you therefore willing to take upon yourself that voluntary obligation?”

Whilst this description gives little clue to the true nature and significance of the obligation he is about to take, the candidate must affirm his willingness to adhere to it beforehand, thus foolishly putting his trust in man. Here the Order unfairly demands adherence to an oath the contents of which the initiate knows nothing about.

No Christian has the right to pledge in advance to keep a vow, the substance and conditions of which he is ignorant. The Reformed Presbyterian Church attacks this sinful practice in the testimony of its church saying, “Membership in Secret Societies involves taking an oath before being aware of the obligation. No man is at liberty to bind his conscience by oath without knowledge of the nature and extent of his obligation.”

Prominent Irish Masonic author George Power in his book ‘A Second Masonic Collection’ defines an obligation: “The root of the word ‘obligation’ is ‘lig’. It means bond, a tie or to be tied together. The prefix of the word is ‘ob’ which means to move toward or to act toward’. Thus we can deduce that *an Obligation is something that moves or acts towards the binding of something together.* Masonically the Obligation has a two-way method of tying things or people together. The Obligation moves towards the joining of the Lodge to the Candidate, and the joining of the candidate to the Lodge” (p. 77).

Some candidates entering the Royal Arch Purple degree may claim some ignorance as to the meaning and grave significance of such an obligation. Nevertheless such naiveté is not shared with the hierarchy of the Royal Arch Purple Chapter. In its book ‘History of the Royal Arch Purple Order’ they assert: “*An obligation is a binding agreement between two or more parties that each will keep his side of the bargain and be faithful to his words*” (p. 192). Like all secret societies the Royal Arch Purple employs ‘the obligation’ as a subtle instrument for uniting the candidate to the Chapter.

the obligation

The solemn obligation begins: “***I ——— ———— do most***

voluntarily, solemnly and sincerely declare that I will never reveal unlawfully, but will ever conceal, the proceedings of my brother Royal Arch Purple men in Chapter assembled, nor will I disclose any matter or thing therein communicated to me, unless to a brother Royal Arch Purple man, well knowing him to be such, or until I have been duly authorised so to do by the proper and legal authorities, . . . And I furthermore do most solemnly and sincerely declare that I will not write, nor indite, cut, carve, stamp, stain, emboss, or engrave upon anything movable or immovable, whereby the secrets of this degree may become unlawfully known through my unworthiness ..."

The wording of this bond has been taken directly from the first degree of Freemasonry where the candidate swears to "*always hale, conceal and never reveal any part or parts, point or points, of the secrets and mysteries of, or belonging to, free and accepted Masons in Masonry, which have been, shall now, or hereafter may be, communicated to me, unless it be a true and lawful brother or brothers…I further solemnly promise, that I will not write those secrets, print, carve, engrave, or otherwise them delineate, or cause or suffer them to be done so by others, if in my power to prevent it, on anything movable or immovable… that our secrets, arts, and hidden mysteries, may improperly become known through my unworthiness*."

The Royal Arch Purple here binds the initiates to conceal the teaching and practices of the Order, *and never reveal it to anyone save fellow Royal Arch Purple men*. Such secrecy is unscriptural and runs contrary to our Lord's plan for the Church, which was designed to be a just, open and outward-reaching body. Jesus said in Mark 16:15: "**Go ye into all the world, and preach the gospel to every creature**."

Indeed, the Lord says, "**there is nothing covered, that shall not be revealed; and hid, that shall not be known. What I tell you in darkness, that speak ye in light: and what ye hear in the ear, that preach ye upon the housetops**" (Matthew 10:26-27).

The Royal Arch Purple then introduces the Protestant cause, as if to 'Christianise' the obligation. They say: "I will to the utmost of my power support and maintain the Protestant religion, and glorious Constitution of 1688, against all foes, foreign and domestic. I will aid and assist all true and faithful Royal Arch Purple men in all just and lawful actions, and I will not wrong, nor see any of them wronged or defrauded, if in my power to prevent it."

The Arch Purple candidate then swears: "***I will not have any unlawful carnal knowledge of a brother Royal Arch Purpleman's wife, mother, daughter, sister, or any of his near or dear female relatives***."

Here, the Royal Arch Purple selectively proscribes one sin, that of unlawful carnal knowledge and then hypocritically applies limits to its extent, namely the female relatives of *its own members*.

We again find the source of such error in Freemasonry where the third degree Mason refers to the female relatives of his brethren in his oath. He vows to "*support a Master Mason's character... and strictly respect the chastity of those who are most dear to him, in the persons of his wife, sister, or his child: and that I will not knowingly have unlawful carnal connexion with any of them*" (Masonic Manual p. 66).

Imagine a believer subjecting himself to such exclusive unscriptural conditions! Taking such a vow to simply abstain from one individual sin is hypocrisy, but qualifying the bounds, to which this sin may be committed against, is an arrogant contravention of God's holy Word.

James 2: 9 -11 says: "**If ye have respect to persons, ye commit sin, and are convinced of the law as transgressors. For whosoever shall keep the whole law, and yet offend in one point, he is guilty of all. For he that said Do not commit adultery, said also, Do not kill. Now if thou commit no adultery, yet if thou kill, thou art become a transgressor of the law**."

Evangelical author Martin L. Wagner, refers to the subject in his book 'Freemasonry - An Interpretation' when he states: "This covenant does not forbid adultery. It aims only to restrict it [and]... while it purposes to protect female virtue, in fact undermines it."

The revival preacher Charles G. Finney in his book 'Character and Claims of Freemasonry' argues that it does not even imply "the semblance of virtue" (p. 44).

Whilst the Royal Arch Purple and Freemasonry are selective in their opposition to sin and discriminating in those to whom it applies, the Word of God is certainly not. Such selective teaching is contrary to the instruction of Scripture and is, in itself, a sin.

The Bible clearly shows that God is no respecter of persons. Romans 2:11 says, "**For there is no respect of persons with God**." Proverbs 28:21 teaches that "**To have respect of persons is not good**." Secret societies should therefore follow God's example and act upon the solemn instruction of His Word.

God hates sin (Romans 1: 18), and cannot look upon it (Habakkuk 1: 13), therefore we have no warrant to be selective in our prohibition or condemnation of it. *Sin is sin.* Professing believers must therefore be consistent in their Christian walk and undiscriminating in their denunciation of wrongdoing.

The hypocrisy of taking such a vow is highlighted by that great man of God, J C Ryle when he says: "If men professing to be converted, and true believers in a crucified Christ, cannot be chaste, self-denying, and obedient without solemnly registering a vow, I must plainly say I think they are not likely to do much good... I think it will be a public confession that they are an inferior order of men" (Charges and Addresses p. 240).

Not only does the Royal Arch Purple obligation break the Law of God, but it also breaks the law of the land. After earlier vowing to "aid and assist" his new brethren in "all just and lawful actions" he is forced to hypocritically swear, ***"I will obey the five points of fellowship, and keep and conceal the secrets of my Royal Arch Purple brethren within my breast, as well as my own, murder and treason excepted."***

This illegal vow, where the Royal Arch Purple candidate binds himself to conceal the secrets of his fellow Arch Purple brethren "murder and treason excepted" is both morally and scripturally wrong. The extent and scale of such concealment is mind-boggling and must be viewed with the greatest concern and abhorrence. So extreme are the legal implications that one wonders how a child of God can offer any justification for such bondage. From manslaughter to rape, incest to robbery, a brother's sin and crimes must be covered up.

The origin of such language is again found within the third degree of Freemasonry when the candidate affirms: "I promise and swear, that I will not speak the Master Mason's word... except... on the five points of fellowship. I promise and swear that a Master Mason's secrets... shall remain secure... *murder and treason excepted.*"

The Westminster Confession of Faith (Ch 22 sec 7) states, "No man may vow to do anything forbidden in the Word of God, or what would hinder any duty therein commanded, or which is not in his own power, and for the performance whereof he hath no promise of ability from God..."

Charles G. Finney says of this sinful Masonic oath, "It is self-evident that this Master's oath is either a conspiracy against the execution of law, or Master Masons care nothing for the solemnity of an oath" (Character and Claims of Freemasonry p. 44).

The Protestant Truth Society pamphlet on the Royal Arch Purple Order written in 1925 by former Deputy Grand Chaplain of the Grand Orange Lodge of England the Rev. Alexander Roger states: "If clerics aid and abet a contravention of the Law of the Realm what is to be expected of the ordinary lay Orangeman?"

The Lord Jesus Christ solemnly cautions in Matthew 12:36-37: "**That every idle word that men shall speak, they shall give account thereof in the day of judgment. For by thy words thou shalt be justified, and by thy words thou shalt be condemned**."

Here also, like the Freemason, the initiate promises under oath to keep a practice he yet knows nothing of, namely the 'five points of fellowship'. The ignorant candidate will later discover that it is in fact a mock resurrection rite, involving even further bondage. Ironically, this 'rite' is common to nearly every secret society and cult throughout the world today.

The RAP candidate concludes his obligation by blasphemously asking God's blessing upon his unholy vow: ***"O help me, Almighty God, and keep me steadfast in this my solemn vow."***

Some misguided apologists for the Royal Arch Purple have sheepishly argued that the contents of the obligation are not to be taken literally. Nevertheless, to invoke the name of Almighty God in an oath is a very serious matter, and something that is not to be taken lightly. To treat an oath in such a flippant manner clearly contravenes the third commandment, which states: "**Thou shalt not take the name of the LORD thy God in vain; for the LORD will not hold him guiltless that taketh his name in vain**" (Exodus 20:7).

This Royal Arch Purple obligation is *a literal, binding agreement*; therefore no child of God can justify committing himself to such illegal **SINFUL** conditions.

A.W. Tozer once declared: "Although he [Satan] is a dark and sinister foe dedicated to the damnation of humans, I think he knows that it is no use trying to damn a forgiven and justified child of God who is in the Lord's hands. So, it becomes the devil's business to keep the Christian's spirit imprisoned. He knows that the believing and justified Christian has been raised up out of the grave of his sins and trespasses. From that point on, Satan works that much harder to keep us bound and gagged, actually imprisoned in our own grave clothes."

By consenting to this abhorrent oath, the Royal Arch Purple candidate swears to keep and conceal *secrets, practices and teaching* he as yet knows absolutely nothing about. A believer's position is more precarious in that he is not only binding himself to an organisation, but also to its members, most of whom bear no testimony of sins forgiven. This unquestionably violates the teaching of God's Word. James 4:4 says, "**Know ye not that the friendship of the world is emnity with God? whosoever will be a friend of the world is the enemy of God**."

The selfish loyalty demanded by secret societies and the inevitably strong bond of fellowship and loyalty which develops from such a commitment, must surely draw Christians entangled within them away from their first love, the Lord Jesus Christ. As a result, it must inevitably weaken their position within the brotherhood of believers.

The Independent Orange Institution, which owns the Royal Arch Purple degree as its third degree, attempt (in a secret memo released to the membership on the 20th February 1998) to defend this sinful oath. Understandably their defence refers exclusively to the part of the obligation which refers to the Protestant religion. They say, "it is true that the obligation has a binding influence amongst the members. We are a 'religious and loyal brotherhood' dedicated to the promotion of Protestantism. We have bound ourselves together for that purpose. We despair to think that a professed Evangelical would object to that."

Such a distorted and selective defence of this sinful obligation must be carefully analysed and answered.

Firstly, the Royal Arch Purple obligation primarily binds men to a man-made institution and its members, rather than to the Protestant cause. The exclusive demands of allegiance made by this unscriptural oath of obligation, draws men further away from the body of believers, the Church, rather than closer to it. The consequence of this obligation ultimately means that his commitment to the same is seriously compromised.

Evangelical Tom C. McKenney in addressing the subject of obligations in his book on Freemasonry, 'Please Tell Me', outlines how the initiate "puts himself in the position of swearing to put his loyalty to the Lodge above other commitments of loyalty." Brother in the Lord, this is at variance with the very principles of true biblical Protestantism!

Secondly, Protestantism needs no such sinful bondage to secure a man's commitment to the Reformed Faith. Such a glorious cause is maintained by trusting in Christ and living by His unadulterated Word.

A.L. Allen, one of the twenty most prominent Orangemen consulted for their opinion of the Royal Arch Purple degree between the years 1876 and 1878 said, in complete agreement with the others: "If such things are required to interest members of the Orange Institution to act as a bond (as is alleged), all I can say is, it speaks but little for their genuine Protestantism. In my opinion the kind of Protestant that such an absurd profane farce pleases is the very sort we should be better without."

Thirdly, no Christian can take *secret society* oaths without sinning against Almighty God. Such an obligation contravenes God's holy Word and offends a thrice-holy God. A true child of God cannot truly fulfil this offensive Arch Purple oath!

Galatians 4:9 says, "**But now, after that ye have known God, or rather are known of God, how turn ye again to the weak and beggarly elements, whereunto ye desire again to be in bondage?**"

Secret society obligations are clearly unbiblical and must be renounced. The word renounce means to take strong verbal action to reject, cut off, totally disown, or break the legal right of something. The believer who realises he has taken an oath that violates God's precious Word must repent (turn away from his sin). Leviticus 5:4-6 says, "**If a soul swear, pronouncing with his lips to do evil, or to do good, whatsoever it be that a man shall pronounce with an oath, and *it be hid from him*; when he knoweth of it, then he shall be guilty in one of these. And it shall be, when he shall be guilty in one of these things, that he shall confess that he hath sinned in that thing: And he shall bring his trespass offering unto the LORD for his sin which he hath sinned.**"

Matthew Henry commenting on this passage states: "If a man binds himself by an oath that he will do or not do such a thing and the performance of his oath afterwards proves either unlawful or impracticable, by which he is discharged from the obligation, yet he must bring an offering to atone for his folly in swearing so rashly... The offender must confess his sin and bring his offering; and the offering was not accepted unless it was accompanied with a penitential confession and a humble prayer for pardon."

Here at the very beginning of the ceremony, the Royal Arch Purple Order stands exposed. Whilst craftily deceiving the ignorant candidate beforehand, that there was nothing in this obligation that may prove detrimental to him in life, or hinder him in the duty he owes to God, his country, or himself, they demand an oath that contravenes these very things. It is difficult to avoid the conclusion that this is unadulterated deception!

God's Word refers to the subject of oath taking in general in James 5:12, stating, "**But above all things, my brethren, swear not, neither by heaven, neither by the earth, neither by any other oath: but let your yea be yea; and your nay, nay; lest ye fall into condemnation**."

Jesus said, "**Swear not at all; neither by heaven; for it is God's throne: Nor by the earth; for it is his footstool: neither by Jerusalem; for it is the city of the great King. Neither shalt thou swear by thy head, because thou canst not make one hair white or black. But let your communication be, Yea, yea; Nay, nay: for whatsoever is more than these cometh of evil**" (Matthew 5:34-37).

Many evangelicals have argued over the years that these verses are evidence that all oaths are wrong. Others assume the traditional Reformed position on oaths which is outlined in the Westminster Confession of Faith (Ch 22 sec 3): "*Whosoever taketh an oath, ought duly to consider the weightiness of so solemn an act, and therein to avouch nothing but what he is fully persuaded is the truth. Neither may any man bind himself by oath to anything but what is good and just, and what he believes so to be, and what he is able and resolved to perform. Yet it is a sin to refuse an oath touching any thing that is good and just, being imposed by lawful authority.*"

Whilst debate may continue among evangelicals on the overall subject of oaths there can surely be no justification, from any side, for this sinful neo-Masonic Royal Arch Purple oath.

God's Word admonishes the *true* child of God to: "**Stand fast therefore in the liberty wherewith Christ hath made us free, and be not entangled again with the yoke of bondage**" (Galatians 5:1).

chapter 3

a degrading inauguration

After securing the initiate's undivided loyalty, the Royal Arch Purple candidate is 'made up' for initiation in a practice known within secret societies and the occult world as being **'properly prepared'**. In 'The Meaning of Masonry', prominent Freemason W.L. Wilmshurst explains the significance of such a practice, saying, "*If he be truly a worthy candidate, **'properly prepared'** in his heart and an earnest seeker for the light, the mere fact of his entering such an atmosphere will so impress and awaken his dormant soul faculties as in itself to constitute an initiation and an indelible memory*" (p. 117).

This custom is, in reality, the state of readiness the initiate obtains before receiving mystical enlightenment into a secret body. The candidate could justly be described as being properly prepared for his (counterfeit) new birth experience. Occultist Fredrick Goodman in his book 'Magical Symbols' contends: "*When a man has so **prepared himself** as to achieve insight into the nature of the spiritual realm, then he is said to be an initiate.*"

The oath-bound Royal Arch Purple aspirant is prepared for initiation in typically Masonic manner, by being stripped of much of his clothes. He is divested of his coat and vest, collar and tie, shoes and socks. One shoe is then placed on candidate's left bare foot, and the legs of his trousers rolled up above the knee, his left breast being bare. The candidate is then blindfolded, and a piece of purple ribbon is fastened to the front of the candidate's shirt or other garment.

The Masonic Candidate
(prepared identical to the Arch Purple initiate apart from the rope)
Re-produced by kind permission

The Arch Purple lecture states: "I was neither naked nor clothed, barefooted nor shod, deprived of all moneys, means, and minerals, blindfolded, and led by the hand of a friend to a door."

semi-naked and barefooted

This peculiar practice of stripping the candidate before initiation, whilst overtly humiliating, has a deep spiritual significance. The custom itself goes back to the time of Nimrod, the father of the ancient mysteries. The Rev. Alexander Hislop in his book 'The Two Babylons' (p. 183) explains how Nimrod, before he was cut in pieces, was "*necessarily stripped*" in what was "*a voluntary humiliation.*" He then states, "When, therefore, his suffering was over, and his humiliation past, the clothing in which he was invested was regarded as a meritorious clothing, available not only for himself, but for all who were initiated in the mysteries."

This obscene rite, consequently, took on great importance within the mysteries and the occult world. Hislop, referring to a typical initiation, states, "after being duly prepared by magic rites and ceremonies, they were ushered, in a state of absolute nudity, into the innermost recesses of the temple" (p. 183).

Hislop then explains, "When the initiated, thus 'illuminated' and made partakers of a 'divine nature', after being 'divested of their garments', were clothed anew, the garments with which they were invested were looked upon as 'sacred garments', and possessing distinguished virtues. 'The coat of skin' with which the Father of mankind was divinely invested after he was made so painfully sensible of his nakedness, was, as all intelligent theologians admit, a typical emblem of the glorious righteousness of Christ - 'the garment of salvation', which is 'unto all and upon all them that believe'. The garments put upon the initiated after their disrobing of their former clothes, were evidently intended as a *counterfeit* of the same" (p. 183). This vulgar practice has assumed a strategic place in most heathen initiations, being subtly designed to mimic the Christian new birth experience.

Freemasonry makes no secret of the significance of such a practice. Masonic authority A.E.Waite in his book 'A New Encyclopaedia of Freemasonry' explains that this preparation is designed to portray "*an image of coming out from some old condition by being unclothed therefrom-partially at least-and thereafter of entering into another and new order, in which a different quality of light is communicated, another vesture is to be assumed and-ultimately-another life entered*" (p. 155).

Clearly, the Arch Purple initiate by participating in such a ceremony is aligning himself with those initiated into the mysteries throughout the centuries. This practice, which harmonises with the rest of the initiation, is carefully devised to caricature the humble and unworthy way a repentant sinner comes to Christ. This objectionable preparation serves not only to divest a man of his clothes but also of his dignity and is designed to represent the putting off of the old garments, the old life and the putting on of the new. Such imagery is intended to undermine the teaching of Scripture, which commands the believer to put off the old man, the old nature, the old lifestyle and "**put on the new man, which after God is created in righteousness and true holiness**" (Ephesians 4:24).

Experienced Freemason Bernard E. Jones in his book 'Freemasons' Guide and Compendium' outlines the mystical significance of entering the lodge bare-footed. He states, "The nations of antiquity worshipped their gods bare-footed and we know that in connexion with religious and magical rites the Romans often had their feet bare… the sorceresses, intent on the exercise of their art, went with one foot or both feet naked... People attended the worship of Isis with naked feet" (p. 269).

To justify this pagan practice the Royal Arch Purple subtly re-enact Moses' encounter with Almighty God at the burning bush, where the candidate is significantly instructed to cast off his shoe, because, as he later learns: "the place whereon I stood was holy ground."

In the 'Symbolism of Freemasonry' (pp. 127-129), the Mason is taught that *the Lodge is the 'holy of holies', it is 'holy ground'*, thus deceptively taking Moses' encounter at the burning bush as justification for their mode of dress. The Royal Arch Purple also conveniently covers such superstitious behaviour with biblical language so as to sweeten the devil's poisonous tablet and cause the initiate to feel comfortable with this iniquity.

The draft to the Royal Arch Purple Chapter book 'History of the Royal Arch Purple Order' says, "Neither barefoot nor shod is a condition which has always been symbolic. In medieval folklore the unlaced shoe was taken as a sign that one was always ready to avert or escape from danger… To remove and give the shoe to another person denoted trust, sincerity and fidelity."

The Chapter attempts to further justify this peculiar heathen practice in the published book, stating, "It is indeed taken as a sign of respect all over the world as seen by the rows of shoes outside mosques." Following Islam's example can hardly be a reason why any Protestant (never mind believer) should take off his shoes in front of a Chapter of largely unregenerate men.

deprived of all moneys

The candidate is deprived of all valuables before participating in initiation, signifying his present poverty-stricken state and his new dependence and trust upon the Chapter. Authoritative Mason Bernard E. Jones explains, in his 'Freemasons' Guide and Compendium' that, "the candidate is deprived of moneys, metallic substances, and of 'everything valuable' before he enters the lodge, so that, emblematically, he is received into masonry poor and penniless, *a symbolism which we might regard as being all-sufficient*" (p. 267).

The Royal Arch Purple Chapter boldly asserts in its unpublished draft that: "The phrases 'neither naked nor clothed' and 'deprived of all moneys, means and minerals' are self-explanatory. They are used to illustrate that *all must be prepared to enter in humility and in a poverty stricken attitude*."

blindfolded

One of the most prominent items within the Royal Arch Purple degree is the blindfold or hoodwink. It has been used by all secret societies throughout the centuries. It is placed on every Arch Purple candidate at the commencement of his initiation and remains on him throughout his travel until its removal at a strategic moment in the ceremony.

The blindfold's significance is distinctly profane and highlights the deception that has been perpetrated by the Royal Arch Purple and the Independent Orange Institution over the years. Like all the mysteries, the blindfold upon the initiate represents 'the spiritual darkness of his soul'. This emblem and its removal later in the ceremony represent the candidate's 'journey from darkness into spiritual enlightenment'.

This is one of Freemasonry's most important objects. Masonic authority Pearson explains: "*The material darkness which is produced by the hoodwink is the emblem of the darkness of the soul.*" ('Christ the Christian and Freemasonry' p. 88)

Mystical initiations must always take place in a mode of darkness. Albert Mackey, thirty-third degree Mason and Masonic historian explains in 'The Craft and its Symbols' (p. 42), that "the aspirant was always kept... in a condition of darkness. Darkness, in all forms of initiation, has always symbolised ignorance" ('Christ the Christian and Freemasonry' p. 88).

The significance of this repulsive occultic emblem is further explained in 'The Pocket Encyclopaedia of Masonic Symbols': "*Blindfolding a candidate in any rite is not for practical but for spiritual reasons. The temporary* The *blinding is a symbol of present darkness, which will be displaced by light when and if the initiate succeeds in penetrating the mysteries before him*" ('Hidden Secrets of the Eastern Star' p. 222).

As in the ancient mysteries, the modern day initiate's journey 'from darkness to light' is a counterfeit of the Christian new birth experience. Modern Masonic writer George Draffin states that that the hoodwink or blindfold in the ritual is to remind the candidate that he is "*undergoing a birth process,*" just as *"conception and fertilisation take place in the darkness of the womb*" ('Inside the Brotherhood' p. 143).

Harry L. Haywood further states: "The purpose of the hoodwink is not to conceal something from the candidate, for it has another significance: it symbolises the fact that *the candidate is yet in darkness, like the babe lying in its mother's womb. Being in darkness the candidate is expected to prepare his inmost mind for those revelations that will be made to him after the hoodwink is removed*" ('Hidden Secrets of the Eastern Star' p. 223).

Some rank and file evangelicals within the Royal Arch Purple might be surprised at such assertions but their hierarchy are certainly not. In the recent Royal Arch Purple publication 'History of the Royal Arch Purple Order' the Order boasts: " All candidates entering the Institution, do so to some degree in a state of ignorance and so it could be said that ***they are open to be hoodwinked***. But it is in this way that the lesson of dependency on the friend that has been sent to guide them can be most clearly demonstrated."

In the draft of the Royal Arch Purple book the significance of the blindfold is more explicitly outlined: "The blindfold or hoodwink is taken by some to denote secrecy, but it can also be symbolic of dependency on a friend and in ***the state of darkness or ignorance which will be relieved by the true light of knowledge***."

Masonic authority Albert Mackey explains this peculiar teaching in 'A Lexicon of Freemasonry' (p. 68): "*Darkness among Freemasons is emblematical of ignorance; for as our science has technically been called 'Lux', or light, the absence of light must be the absence of knowledge… In the spurious Freemasonry of the ancient mysteries, the aspirant was always shrouded in darkness, as a preparatory step to the reception of the full light of knowledge.*"

child of God subjecting himself to such error and allowing himself to participate in this hoodwinked ceremony (ignorantly or not) is in a dangerous position. He is openly denying the light of the Christian's new birth and blasphemously denying his true Redeemer and the teaching of His precious Word. The Bible says, "**men loved darkness rather than light, because their deeds were evil**" (John 3:19).

The hoodwink has always been used in pagan ceremonies. Its origins stretch back into the mists of time, to the heathen initiations of the ancient mysteries. Masonic authority Harry Haywood states: "The use of the blindfold goes far back among secret societies, even to the ancient mysteries, in which the candidate was usually made to enter the sanctuary with eyes covered. The Cathari, whom [Pope] Innocent III tried so hard to annihilate, and who were at bottom Christian mystics, were accustomed to call those seeking initiation into their mysteries 'hoodwinked slaves' implying that the eyes of the soul were still blind in ignorance and lust" ('Hidden Secrets of the Eastern Star' p. 222).

The Bible states: "**If we say that we have fellowship with him** [Christ], **and walk in darkness, we lie, and do not the truth: But if we walk in the light, as he is in the light, we have fellowship one with another, and the blood of Jesus Christ his Son cleanseth us from all sin**" (I John 1:6-7).

rope *(noose, cable-tow or halter)* around the neck

The Masonic practice of placing a rope round the neck of the prepared candidate does not exist within the Royal Arch Purple Chapter of Ireland. Nevertheless the Chapter's book, 'History of the Royal Arch Purple Order' does refer to an undated document from the Grand Orange Lodge of England (which must be post 1913, when English Orangeism accepted the Arch Purple into their Institution). They compare it to the Irish working of the Arch Purple. The Chapter's book states, "There is one major variation in this degree, that is in the instruction for the preparing a candidate, a halter [a rope] is to be placed around his neck," and they continue, "This must have been a local practice as it is not spoken of in any other place and certainly not usual in Ireland" (p. 185).

So what is the significance of this custom? Here again we must go behind the Masonic veil of secrecy to discover the meaning of this strange usage. In the Masonic first degree the 'Worshipful Master' explains to the blindfolded candidate how there was a "Cable Tow, with a running noose about your neck, which would have rendered any attempt to retreat ... fatal by strangling" (Masonic Manual p. 9). Every aspect of preparation and instruction, so subtly inherited from Freemasonry, is devilishly designed to draw men into the bondage of fear.

Martin Short in his book 'Inside the Brotherhood' outlines the spiritual significance of the cable-tow round the candidate, stating that "the cable-tow round his neck is 'a symbolical umbilical cord' which when cut, symbolizes 'birth and new life' " (p. 143).

summary

Like all secret societies the mode of preparation for initiation into the Royal Arch Purple is subtly designed by the devil to mimic the humble, unworthy and totally dependent state in which a repentant sinner comes to Christ for salvation.

Whilst the Arch Purple Order causes its candidate to humble themselves in the presence of the Chapter the Bible admonishes man: "**Humble yourselves therefore under the mighty hand of God, that he may exalt you in due time**" (1 Peter 5:6).

The Protestant Truth Society booklet written by former Deputy Grand Chaplain of the Grand Orange Lodge of England, Rev. Alexander Roger, states: "*Is it becoming to a Christian man and the self respect of any gentleman to appear in this half stripped condition? Is it necessary in order to secure his adherence to the maintenance of the Protestant Faith in Church and State to enforce submission to what after all is a degrading ceremony bordering upon the blasphemous? That it should be deemed necessary to blindfold the Candidate until nearly the close of the initiation is strongly suggestive.*"

As we analyse the pathetic sight of the prepared Royal Arch Purple candidate, we see a remarkable picture of the carnal Laodicean Church described in Revelation 3. The Lord condemned it, saying: "thou art *wretched, and miserable,* ***and poor, and blind, and naked***" (V. 17). This vivid betrayal, which is shared with most other secret societies and occult bodies throughout the world, shows the incredible lengths to which Satan will go, to mock the Word of God. Could this pitiful mode of preparation be a graphic picture of the dismal spiritual state of the Church in Ulster today?

Surely when upwards of 95,000 Ulster Protestant males can be lured into such an undignified state to join a so-called Protestant Order we are in urgent need of God's help.

Jesus says of the Laodiceans, "**thou art neither cold nor hot: I would thou wert cold or hot. So then because thou art lukewarm, and neither cold nor hot, I will spue thee out of my mouth** " (Revelation 3:15-16).

The Protestant people of Ulster seem to be under the judgement of God. Surely it is time for us to get back to the old trusted paths of our forefathers and consecrate our lives afresh to the Saviour.

The Lord instructs the believer: **"I counsel thee to buy of me gold tried in the fire, that thou mayest be rich; and white raiment, that thou mayest be clothed, and that the shame of thy nakedness do not appear; and anoint thine eyes with eyesalve, that thou mayest see. As many as I love, I rebuke and chasten: be zealous therefore, and repent**" (Revelation 3:18-19).

Brother in the Lord, remember that "**judgment must begin at the house of God**" (1 Peter 4:17).

chapter 4

a hostile reception

After his oath-binding and preparation, the hoodwinked, semi–naked candidate is led to the Chapter door by a conductor, who is assigned to lead him through his travel. This specially selected guide will be at his side for the duration of his initiation and will lead the initiate into what can only be described for him as a journey into the unknown. Here the humbled candidate places himself in the control of the conductor/guide for direction, thus once again putting his trust in man.

Informed sources within the Royal Arch Purple Chapter would estimate that 5 to 10% of the Order, truly profess Christ although this figure would be a lot higher in the Independent Orange. The average initiate into the Arch Purple is therefore *normally* in no better a spiritual state than the guide leading him. These conductors most of whom, bear no testimony of sins forgiven are no better than modern day Pharisees, whom Christ rebuked: "**Woe unto you, ye blind guides** " (Matthew 23:16).

Our Saviour described such ambassadors of empty religion as "**blind leaders of the blind**," and declared, "**if the blind lead the blind, both shall fall into the ditch**" (Matthew 15:14).

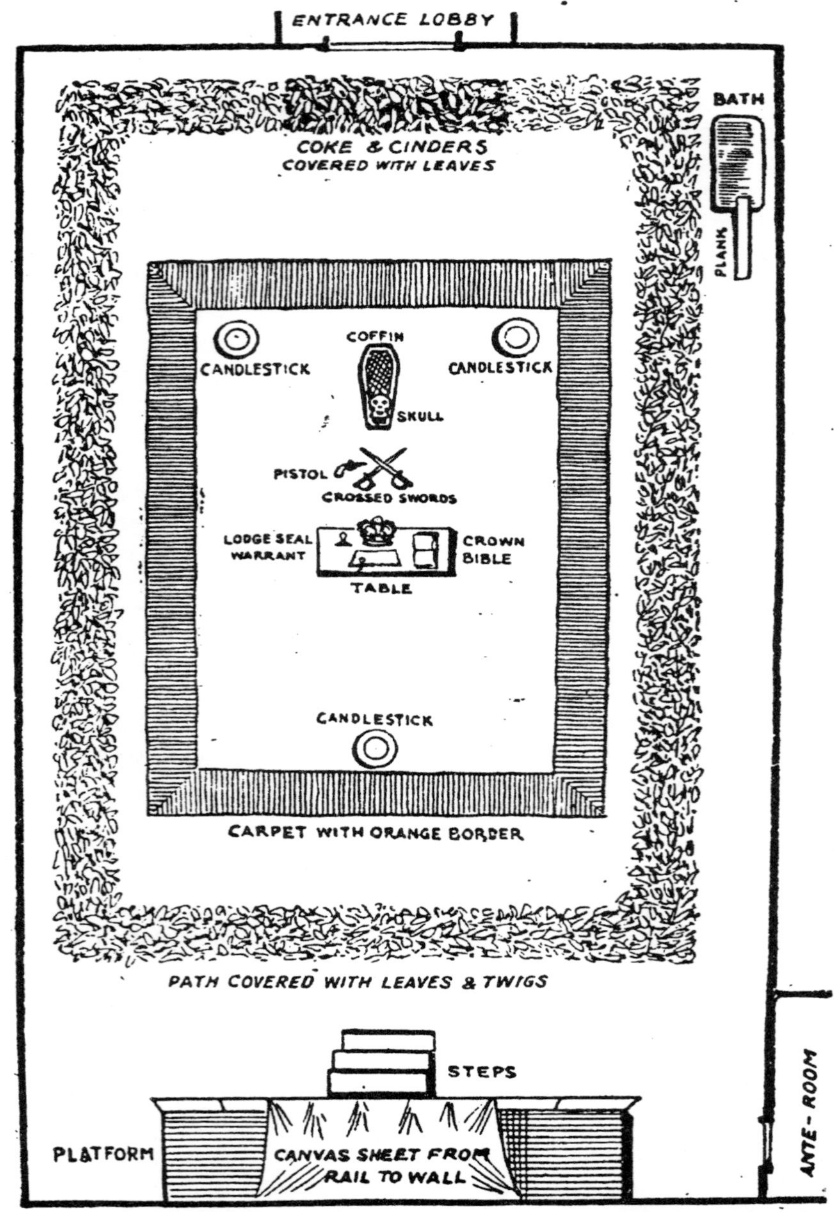

PLAN OF LODGE ROOM FOR ROYAL ARCH PURPLE DEGREE

Re-produced by kind permission of the Protestant Truth Society

the profane

The guide then knocks three times on the Chapter door seeking entry. The time-honoured response from within the Arch Purple assembly defies normal belief: "***What profane, or unworthy person or persons are these, coming here to disturb the peace and harmony of this, our Royal Arch Purple Chapter meeting dedicated by us unto God, and Brother Joshua?***"

Like all the mysteries, those outside the Order are looked upon as profane and unworthy. The implication for any child of God allowing himself to be labelled with such a depraved title must surely undermine the regenerating work of Christ in his life. Moreover it must damage his testimony before his fellow Royal Arch Purple men.

The Chapter door is guarded by a person called a "Tyler" whose responsibility it is to protect the meeting. This practice is in keeping with the model of all the ancient mysteries. The 'Master's Carpet' explains: "Initiations into the Ancient Mysteries were performed in caverns, and the entrance was guarded by a janitor armed with a drawn sword to prevent unlawful intrusion" ('Christ the Christian and Freemasonry' p. 87). Not surprisingly, the Arch Purple 'Tyler' is also armed with a sword.

The guide replies to the question from within the Chapter room: "They are not profane, nor unworthy at all, but friends with a brother, and a brother with friends, seeking admission into this, your Royal Arch Purple Chapter meeting, dedicated by you unto God and Brother Joshua." Here the reason for their worthiness and acceptance is the correct response of the guides, and their Royal Arch Purple membership.

The English word 'profane' is derived from the Latin word 'profanis', meaning 'before or outside the temple, hence not holy, not clean, debased and unworthy, a thing to be avoided for it would contaminate the holy and clean ones'.

One can nearly hear an apologist for the Order saying this is not what is meant by the Royal Arch Purple. Nevertheless in their recent publication (p. 192) the Royal Arch Purple Chapter unashamedly declare: "*When greeted by the word 'profane' it may leave some people at a loss to understand the meaning. It is not a word which is in common or everyday use. In the context in which it is used here it means the uninitiated, in a religious sense it means a 'heathen' or one 'outside the temple'*." This amazing statement reveals the spurious nature of the Royal Arch Purple Order.

This sinful esoteric practice is not exclusive to the Royal Arch Purple but is shared with most secret societies and occult groups throughout the globe. Leading modern historian and scholar of Freemasonry, thirty-third degree Mason, Albert Mackey explains in a 'Manual of the Lodge' (p. 20): "*There he* [the man to be initiated] *stands, without our portals, on the threshold of his new Masonic life, in darkness, helplessness and ignorance. Having been wandering amid the errors, and covered over with the pollutions of the outer and profane world. He comes inquiringly to our doors, seeking the new birth, and asking a withdrawal of the veil*" ('Deadly Deception' p. 135).

Such a practice, again, has originated from the ancient mysteries. According to Mackey, the Ancient Mysteries commenced ceremonies of the greater initiation by the solemn form of "Depart hence ye profane."

'Profane', of course is a scriptural word used to define an unregenerate person, a child of darkness. Imagine the scene of a blindfolded, bare breasted, bare-legged child of God being led to the door of a room full of largely unsaved men, then subjecting himself to the position of an unworthy sinner in need of light.

As we turn to God's Word, one cannot help but see history repeating itself. In the book of Ezekiel we learn how the clergy of that day were absorbed in such sin and hypocrisy: "**Her priests have violated my law, and have profaned mine holy things: they have put no difference between the holy and profane, neither have they showed the difference between the unclean and the clean, and have hid their eyes from my Sabbaths, and I am profaned among them**" (Ezekiel 22: 26).

There is no ambiguity with God as regards what is, and who is, profane. Scripture clearly describes the profane. Esau is given as an example of a 'profane' person in Scripture. Hebrews 12: 16 says: "Lest there be any fornicator, or profane person, as Esau, who for one morsel of meat sold his birthright." As most believers know Esau became the focus of God's wrath. Romans 9:13 states: "As it is written, Jacob have I loved, but Esau have I hated."

The Royal Arch Purple conceals its vulgar teaching beneath a facade of neo-religious terminology. This language, which often appears ambiguous, is common to all secret societies and is known as esoteric (or hidden) teaching. An example is seen as follows:

Q. ***"Where are you from?***
A. ***The outer Camp of Israel [the profane world].***
Q. ***Where are you going?***
A. ***To the inner lines [the elect].***
Q. ***How do you intend to get there?***
A. ***By the benefit of a password.***
Q. ***Have you that password?***
A. ***I have.***
Q. ***Will you give it to me?***
A. ***I will, if you begin - Shib - Bo - Leth.***

William T. Still in his book 'New World Order' reveals the Masonic source of this password stating: "In the second degree, or 'fellowcraft degree', the candidate enters the lodge by the benefit of the secret password 'Shibboleth' and takes additional oaths" (p. 103).

sword prick

As the Royal Arch Purple candidate enters the Chapter room, a sword or other sharp object is pressed into his bare breast. The Protestant Truth Society booklet of 1925 revealed: "The oath taken, the candidate is branded with the Seal of the Lodge upon his bare chest - the seal, if a metal one, having been previously heated for the impression." The reason for such an action is explained during the Royal Arch Purple lecture.

Q. ***"How were you admitted? Or upon what?***
A. ***On the point of a sword, spear, or some other warlike instrument pointed to my naked left breast.***
Q. ***Why to your naked left breast?***
A. ***Because it was nearest my heart.***

Q.	***Did you feel anything?***
A.	***Three sharp pricks to my naked left breast.***
Q.	***What did these three sharp pricks to your naked left breast signify?***
A.	***As they were a prick to my flesh in the meantime, so may they be a sting to my conscience hereafter, if ever I should divulge anything I had received or was about to receive.*** "

The significance of this practice is solemnly outlined during the Masonic first degree initiation, when the candidate is told: "At your entrance into the Lodge, this sword was presented to your naked left breast, so that had you rashly attempted to rush forward, you would have been accessory to your own death by stabbing. Not so with the brother who held it; as he would have only remained firm to his duty" (Masonic Manual p. 9).

We learn in the 'Freemasons' Guide and Compendium' that by the candidate enduring such a reception, "There is brought home to him the seriousness of the step which he proposes to take, and he is reminded of the responsibility that will rest on him to guard the secrets about to be entrusted to him" (p. 273).

Describing the Arch Purple ceremony, Tony Gray, in his book 'The Orange Order' reveals that, a certain Frank A. Preble from Waltham, Massachusetts, U.S.A., whilst being initiated was "burned on the breast with a branding iron, which gave him wounds which were raw for some ten days afterwards."

This offensive practice is common to all occult bodies and is designed to intimidate the disorientated candidate, filling him with great fear. Its prime aim is to protect and secure the sinful selfish secrets and mysteries of this objectionable Order. Nevertheless, the Bible says, "**God hath not given us the spirit of fear; but of power, and of love, and of a sound mind**" (2 Timothy 1:7).

Former Wiccan Witch high priest and thirty-second degree Freemason, William J Schnoebelen in comparing the remarkable similarities between Freemasonry and the initiation into witchcraft, exposes the satanic home of this practice. He states that both groups "Challenge the candidate by piercing their naked chest with a sharp instrument (witches use a sword, Masons, the point of a compass)." In the 'History of Initiation' by Oliver, we find the origins of this ancient practice in the Persian mysteries where the initiates were met by the point of the sword being pressed into their left breast.

unexpected bang

The blindfolded candidate is further disturbed by a loud and unexpected bang. This surprise can take many forms and often differs from area to area. One Chapter may fire a blank round from a gun at the initiate, another may smash a set of cymbals, another may simply drop the poles of the lodge's banner on the floor beside him and others use different means. Regardless of the method or the means the aim of the Chapter is always to unsettle the unsuspecting candidate and reduce him to a vulnerable condition. From a medical perspective this behaviour is highly dangerous, but from a spiritual standpoint this performance is deeply offensive. The Chapter seems to justify this foul practice, in its lecture, by claiming Divine approval:

Q "What did you hear?
A. A loud report, as of a cannon-gun, or some other small piece of musketry.
Q. What did this loud report signify?
A. The Lord thundering down his wrath upon the children of Israel for their disobedience unto him."

The disoriented candidate is then forced to his knees, where he is *required* to '***pray for his own deliverance***'.

Whilst the Chapter offers its candidate nothing more than fear, devious threats, and subtle intimidation, the Lord comes to give men peace, love and joy. Jesus said, "**Peace I leave with you, my peace I give unto you: not as the world giveth, give I unto you. Let not your heart be troubled, neither let it be afraid**" (John 14:27).

chapter 5

a humiliating travel

The Royal Arch Purple candidate is led round the Chapter room three times in a time-honoured heathen manner. This practice is known as 'circumambulation' and is common to all the pagan ancient mysteries and all their modern day counterparts. Albert Mackey describes, in 'A Lexicon of Freemasonry' (p. 57): "Circumambulation or a procession around the altar, always formed a part of the ancient religious ceremonies [the ancient mysteries]."

In his Manual of the Lodge, (p. 24) Mackey says that: "Circumambulation among pagan nations referred to... sun worship. Freemasonry alone has preserved the primitive meaning."

Irish Masonic authority and author George Power in his book 'A 2nd Masonic Collection' (p. 56) expounds the pagan origins of circumambulation: "In Degree and Installation ceremonies, we are familiar with the custom of processing around the altar. This derives from one of the most ancient religious ceremonies. In ancient Greece, the priests walked three times round the altar during sacrifice, and sang a sacred hymn. The procession moved according to the course of the sun, and a hymn to Apollo had words 'We imitate the example of the sun, and follow its benevolent course'. The Druid priests used a similar ceremony - three times round the altar, accompanied by all the worshippers. In the Scottish Isles, the people, in religious ceremonies, walked three times round the cairns. All these processions were in a clockwise direction, east to west, according to the course of the sun...we should be conscious of the solemn and mysterious custom which stretches back to the dawn of civilisation."

It is amazing to see how such a blatant heathenish practice could infiltrate an institution professing Protestantism. The same shows how easily men can be deceived.

Whilst ignorance may pervade throughout the grassroots of the Royal Arch Purple about such matters, those in authority within the Order share no such naivete. In the draft copy of the Royal Arch Purple book 'History of the Royal Arch Purple Order', the Chapter states: "The part of the degree which we refer to as the 'travel' is where the original theme is played out. It is conducted in a time honoured manner, namely by 'circumambulation' or walking all around. *This is a practice that has been used from very early times in all the mysteries and religions of every age*. It was usual to walk all around a sacred object or place in a very formal manner. The Romans observed this custom for expiation and purification and their word 'Lustratio' implies purification and walking in a circular direction always in a clockwise direction." How long will the membership be deceived!

The Royal Arch Purple candidate circumambulates the Chapter room three times, the floor of which is covered in branches and brambles, so as to ensure the journey is one of obvious suffering for the barefooted candidate.

The floor covering may vary slightly from Chapter to Chapter, but the ceremony is usually the same. The Protestant Truth Society's pamphlet of 1925 describes the scene of a helpless initiate's journey across a Chapter floor covered in hot coals: "The unfortunate candidate stepping upon the coke and cinders uttered exclamations of pain and surprise. He fell to the floor upon coke-amid renewed laughter. The coke was imported into the ceremony (so the Master said) as a 'special treat' for the unfortunate candidate." This sinister practice is widely employed throughout eastern religion.

Deuteronomy 18:10-12 solemnly warns, "**There shall not be found among you any one that maketh his son or his daughter to pass through the fire, or that useth divination, or an observer of times, or an enchanter, or a witch, Or a charmer, or a consulter with familiar spirits, or a wizard, or a necromancer. For all that do these things are an**

abomination unto the LORD: and because of these abominations the LORD thy God doth drive them out from before thee."

During his three journeys round the Chapter room, the candidate (without warning) is violently whipped on his legs with brambles and branches by the assembled brethren. This practice normally results in varying amounts of cuts and bruises to the initiate, depending on the brethren administering such, the candidate enduring a symbolic fall, each lap of the hall.

The Painful Travel
(Drawn by G. Evans)

The whipping of the initiate's legs and the barefooted travel over brambles and branches is painfully endured by the candidate to the accompaniment of hilarious laughter from all those present, many imitating goat bleats, (reminding the candidate of his impending ride on the goat). This deeply offensive practice is carefully designed to further humiliate the nervous candidate. Amazingly, such ridiculous buffoonery is accompanied by the reading of Holy Scripture. The Protestant Truth Society's pamphlet of

1925 again testifies to such, stating: "The Chaplain during this portion as other portions of the ceremony, is engaged in either reading portions of Scripture or certain prayers."

Like all secret societies the Royal Arch Purple Order preside over the hypocritical large scale appointing of scores of unsaved men to the office of 'Chaplain'. Whilst some so-called separated ministers within the Royal Arch Purple Order are quick to deride the mainline churches for placing unconverted men into office, they themselves are condoning the same by their active participation in the Royal Arch Purple. Such behaviour wherever it occurs is unscriptural and is more akin to the sinful actions of disobedient King Jeroboam in Scripture who "**made priests of the lowest of the people, which were not of the sons of Levi**" (I Kings 12:31).

This apostate practice only serves to deceive godless men into feeling a false sense of righteousness and respectability. Jesus aptly said of such men: "**Ye hypocrites, well did Esaias prophesy of you, saying, This people draweth nigh unto me with their mouth, and honoureth me with their lips; but their heart is far from me. But in vain they do worship me, teaching for doctrines the commandments of men**" (Matthew 15:7-9).

Clearly, the reading of God's Word is not to be taken lightly and is certainly no laughing matter. No Order, whatever its label, has the authority to treat the Bible in such an irreverent manner. Those involved in such mockery should pay heed to the solemn words of Scripture. The Bible says, "**Cleanse your hands, ye sinners; and purify your hearts, ye double minded. Be afflicted, and mourn, and weep: let your laughter be turned to mourning and your joy to heaviness. Humble yourselves in the sight of the Lord, and he shall lift you up**" (James 4:8-10).

In trying to justify this humiliating experience, the Royal Arch Purple employ the scriptural story where the children of Israel journeyed through the wilderness. The lecturer states: "I was led three times around the wilderness, once across the Red Sea, and the river Jordan, to testify that I was duly prepared to receive the degree of a Royal Arch Purple man."

The roots of such folly are again found in Freemasonry where the Royal Arch candidate is told, "As Moses led the Chosen People in their devious wanderings through the wilderness, so I now conduct you."

In normal circumstances the perpetrators of such an organised scandal would find themselves subject to the civil or criminal law, and facing widespread public ridicule. Notwithstanding, such folly exposes the rogue nature of the Royal Arch Purple. In a spiritual context this indecent ceremony violates the conduct expected of a child of God in a Christian gathering. The Bible says: "**Let all things be done decently and in order**" (1 Corinthians 14:40).

The Arch Purple lecturers later poetically explain, "I was beaten and torn by brier and bramble, bitten and stung by fiery serpents, I received three great and mighty falls with my back to the earth, and my face towards the heavens."

In 'The Origins of Freemasonry' by David Stevenson, we discover the significance of such a ceremony: "The element of rough horseplay and humiliation commonly found in these types of ceremony...may be undignified, but formed important elements in the ritual with serious functions...those who had to suffer to gain entry were more likely to be strongly committed to the group they had joined than they would otherwise have been. The ordeal at once indicated to the candidate how exclusive the new status was and that he had to be proved worthy of it...The fact that all in a group had to undergo the same type of initiation served to create a strong bond between them. But there was also another psychological effect associated with the elements of ordeal. Stress may be deliberately induced to heighten receptivity to new ideas...Fear and pain (either physical, or psychological pain induced by having to accept ritual humiliation) can be aids to memory."

He then reveals, "The ordeals of entry to mystery cults in the ancient world had exploited pain, fear, humiliation and exhaustion as aids to changing attitudes, just as modern brain-washing techniques do."

The Royal Arch Purple Chapter tries to excuse this behaviour in the draft copy to its book, stating it exists to, "*denote the seriousness of the step he is about to take and remind him and the members, of the responsibility that rests with them to keep a constant guard against those who would work against the best interests of the members.*" This statement reveals the pathetic attitude that exists within this sinful Order.

The Royal Arch Purple shows little respect for the dignity of its members when they reduce them to such a pitiable state. Furthermore, for a Christian to subject himself to such indignity in front of men (who are largely unsaved) from his own neighbourhood must seriously damage his testimony. One wonders how he could expound (with any credence) the *solemn truths* of God's Word to his 'new found brethren' after participating in such a profane farce. The Bible solemnly declares, "**Now we command you, brethren, in the name of our Lord Jesus Christ, that ye withdraw yourselves from every brother that walketh disorderly, and not after the tradition which he received of us. For yourselves know how ye ought to follow us: for we behaved not ourselves disorderly among you** " (II Thessalonians 3:6-7).

Such unseemly behaviour is at variance with the teaching of Scripture, which instructs the believer: "**Let your moderation be known unto all men. The Lord is at hand**" (Philippians 4:5).

The Protestant Truth Society booklet of 1925 asks this important question: "*Can you picture a more discreditable parody of Sacred things, conducted as it was amid efforts of the onlookers to restrain inordinate laughter? Does not this introductory invocation to the Holy Spirit bring it within very close proximity of blasphemy? Think of so-called ministers of the Gospel taking part in such a scene! To countenance it at all is to disgrace their profession and bring discredit upon themselves.*"

Strong opposition to the Royal Arch-Purple degree existed within the Orange Institution throughout the whole of the 19th century. Prominent English Orangeman, Henry Prigg reflected this sentiment when in December 1877 he declared: "*Rites such as the Arch-Purple attract the wrong men into our ranks; we want sober, religious-minded Protestants, not pot-house politicians and practical jokers...Let the Pagan practices be prohibited and put out of the Order, and then men not worth having with their tomfoolery will leave us and go elsewhere, and better men will be attracted to our ranks.*"

five points of fellowship

The three journeys of the candidate round 'the wilderness' are accompanied by three great falls symbolising the candidate's victory over death and the grave. As the candidate is led round the room the first time he sustains a fall, and is raised up, on the words "***O death, where is thy sting***?" He is then led round again and receives the second fall, and is raised up, on the words "***O grave, where is thy victory***?"

The Royal Arch Purple here, foolishly, apply this text, found in 1 Corinthians 15, to *all* its initiates, presenting a false hope of victory over death and the grave. Such hope pertains *solely* to a child of God and should never be addressed to a child of darkness. No amount of manufactured ceremony within the Royal Arch Purple initiation will ever procure victory over death and the grave for man; such comes through Christ alone.

Jesus said, "**Verily, verily, I say unto you, He that heareth my word, and believeth on him that sent me, hath everlasting life, and shall not come into condemnation; but is passed from death unto life** " (John 5:24).

The child of God alone can sing with assurance of Christ:

"To Him I owe my life and breath,
And all the joys I have;
He makes me triumph over death,
He saves me from the grave."

On the third and final lap round the Chapter room, the initiate sustains his third and final fall, which results in him being blasphemously raised to a figurative new birth by the five points of fellowship. This practice involves the candidate being raised from the floor by a lecturer or office bearer, who is assisted by some of the assembled brethren. The 'brother' raising the candidate then embraces him and acts out each individual point of fellowship; so as to leave a deep impression upon the candidate.

As the candidate is raised he is taught:

"*First - Foot to foot. That I would not be afraid nor ashamed to go a foot or two out of my way to serve* ***a brother Royal Arch Purple man*** *in his time of need.*

Second - Knee to knee. That I would not bend my knee in prayer, without remembering ***my Royal Arch Purple brethren*** *in my prayers, as well as myself.*

Third - Hand in hand. That I would go hand in hand with ***my Royal Arch Purple brethren*** *in all just and lawful actions."*

Fourth - Breast to breast, that I would keep and conceal the secrets of ***my Royal Arch Purple brethren*** *within my breast, as well as my own, murder and treason excepted."*

Here the hypocrisy of the Royal Arch Purple is once again exposed. In the one breath the candidate is told to go hand in hand with his brethren in "all just and lawful actions." In the next he is admonished to conceal the secrets of his Royal Arch Purple brethren, "murder and treason excepted." This sinful demand is carefully designed to further remind the candidate of his grave obligation of loyalty, which he undertook to his brethren at the commencement of the ceremony.

"*Fifth and last - Left hand behind back. To testify that I would be as true and faithful behind* ***a Royal Arch Purple man's*** *back as I would be before his face. I would allow no plots nor plans to be laid about him, without giving him due and timely warning of all approaching danger, as far as in my power lieth, so that, on the one hand, he can come manfully forward to meet it, or, on the other hand, step aside and avoid it.*"

The Royal Arch Purple appropriated this sinful practice from pagan Masonry, changing the order of the five points of fellowship slightly. The Masonic sequence follows -

First - Hand in hand ...

Second - Foot to foot ...

Third - Knee to knee ...

Fourth - Breast to breast...

Fifth and last - Hand over back ...

The extent and gravity of loyalty demanded by the 'five points of fellowship' can never be met by a true child of God. His real brethren are not those who share the same polluted collarette, but those of the household of faith. This selfish, sinful allegiance demanded by the Royal Arch Purple violates the teaching of Christ, who said: "**For whosoever shall do the will of my Father which is in heaven, the same is my brother, and sister, and mother**" (Matthew 12:50).

What is the will of the Father?

The Lord explains in John 6:40: "**And this is the will of him that sent me, that every one which seeth the Son, and believeth on him, may have everlasting life**."

For the committed Christian, a brother is a fellow believer, one who has surrendered his life to Christ. Such exclusive loyalty to a sinful, man-made brotherhood with its many unsaved members is a clear contravention of Scripture and an anathema to the faith. James 4:4 says: "**know ye not that friendship of the world is enmity with God?**"

resurrection

Whilst the exclusive language of the five points of fellowship is clearly objectionable to evangelicals, it is the figurative resurrection rite that accompanies it which proves probably one of the most idolatrous practices found within secret societies.

That which the Arch Purple often conceals, Freemasonry normally reveals. Even allowing for Masonry's veiled language, there is usually enough explanation given in their ceremony to give the discerning candidate some indication of the true significance of the Order's practices.

After being raised on the five points of fellowship in the third degree, the Master Mason learns, "*It is thus all Master Masons are raised from a figurative death to a reunion with the former companions of their toils... Yet even by this feeble ray you may perceive that you stand on the very brink of the grave into which you have figuratively descended*" (Masonic Manual p. 70).

Every practice employed within secret societies is carefully designed to counterfeit and undermine important elements within the Christian new birth. As we analyse these superstitious five points of fellowship, we discover a subtle design to mimic the biblical practice of believers' baptism.

Romans 6:3-8 explains the important symbolic significance of believers' baptism and its relationship to the new birth: "**Know ye not, that so many of us as were baptized into Jesus Christ were baptized into his death? Therefore we are buried with him by baptism into death: that like as Christ was raised up from the dead by the glory of the Father, even so we also should walk in newness of life. For if we have been planted together in the likeness of his death, we shall be also in the likeness of his resurrection: Knowing this, that our old man is crucified with him, that the body of sin might be destroyed, that henceforth we should not serve sin. For he that is dead is freed from sin. Now if we be dead with Christ, we believe that we shall also live with him**."

We clearly see that this corrupt Arch Purple practice, which is shared with many modern secret societies and cults, is in reality a grim mockery of the Christian new birth experience. In the 'Manual of the Lodge', by Albert Mackey (1862) we learn, "*The Master Mason represents a man saved from the grave of iniquity, and raised to the faith of salvation.*"

W.J. McK. McCormick in 'Christ, the Christian and Freemasonry' explains: "He [the candidate] falls under the blows of the 'Assassins' and, shamming death, is 'buried'. Some Lodges are constructed with a grave in the floor, into which the candidate is lowered ... Well, after death and burial comes the 'resurrection'. Two attempts are made to raise 'the corpse' and 'prove a slip'. The Worshipful Master then leaves the chair to show how it can be achieved. He embraces the 'corpse' with the 'five points of fellowship' (breast to breast, knee to knee, etc.) and the 'corpse' returns to life. The candidate's baser nature is now dead and he rises a perfectly regenerated being" (p. 36).

This heathenish practice can ultimately be traced back to the pagan religion of Egypt and the elevation of their false gods, Osiris, Isis and Horus. Egyptian religion being built around the mythical life, death, and 'resurrection' of Osiris.

Martin Short in his secular book, 'Inside The Brotherhood' affirms that, "Osiris was a King of Egypt who married his sister Isis. His brother, Set, wished to usurp the throne and so plotted his death. He tricked Osiris into climbing in a golden chest. As soon as he was inside, Set nailed down the lid and flung the chest into the Nile. It was carried off to Byblos in Syria where it came to rest against a small tamarisk or acacia tree, with the dead Osiris still inside. Isis found out what Set had done to Osiris, so she set off to find her husband."

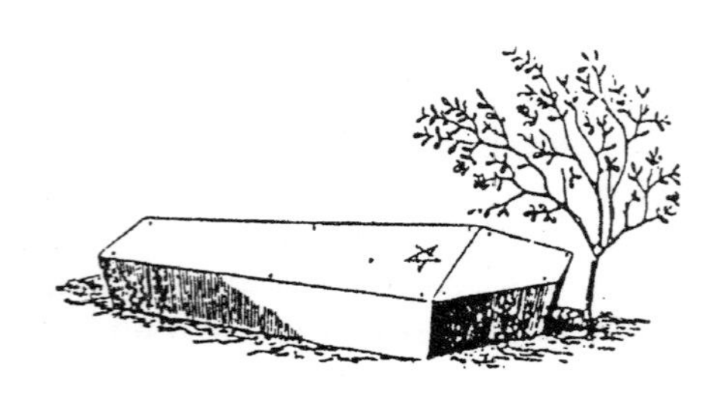

He continues, "A vision led her to Byblos, where she recovered his body and took it back to Egypt. Alas! Set stole it and tore it into fourteen pieces, which he scattered through Egypt to prevent Osiris coming to life again. Isis recovered all but one of the pieces and gave Osiris a fit burial. Their son, Horus, avenged him by slaying Set. Another son Anubis, resurrected Osiris with the lion grip. Having triumphed over the grave, Osiris now reigns as King and Judge of the so-called dead."

This Egyptian trinity is always personified in pagan art by the sun (with a face), the moon (with a face), and the all-seeing eye.

Evangelical authority, former occult High Priest and thirty-second degree Freemason William Schnoebelen, alludes to this practice, revealing, "This a blatant re-creation of the ancient pagan sex-cult resurrection rites...and a mockery of the Lord's resurrection and Christian baptism! After 'dying' with the Masonic 'christ' (actually Baal or Tammuz), he is raised with him... The resurrection... is intended to be what occultists call a 'conscience-raising experience'. It is supposed to induce an altered state of consciousness, an open doorway for demon oppression" (p. 222).

Whilst this deceptive, superstitious rite is designed by the devil to counterfeit the Christian new birth experience, the child of God can joyfully testify to being delivered from death unto everlasting life through faith in the Lord Jesus Christ alone. The Bible says: "**But God, who is rich in mercy, for his great love wherewith he loved us, Even when we were dead in sins, hath quickened us together with Christ, (by grace ye are saved;) And hath raised us up together, and made us sit together in heavenly places in Christ Jesus**" (Ephesians 2:4-6).

The true believer stands blameless before the throne of grace, being justified by faith and born again of the Spirit of God. The hand of God rather than the tainted arm of flesh has graciously raised him up to a marvellous newness of life. The Bible says: "**There is therefore now no condemnation to them which are in Christ Jesus, who walk not after the flesh, but after the Spirit. For the law of the Spirit of life in Christ Jesus hath made me free from the law of sin and death**" (Romans 8:1-2).

chapter 6

a mysterious ascent

The blindfolded Royal Arch Purple candidate is led over to within four or five feet of the front of a purpose-built ladder, symbolising 'Jacob's ladder'. The candidate then steps 'two and a half' paces forward towards the ladder, in an observance called 'the advancement'. The Royal Arch Purple draft explains, "This 'advancement' by steps is not unique to the Arch Purple but is shared by the Masonic Order." This 'two and a half' paces represent the secret mystical number of the Order. This mystical number permeates through all aspects of Arch Purple secrecy.

The Protestant Truth Society booklet of 1925 reveals the significance of the two and a half, stating, "They [The Royal Arch Purple] claim to be representative of the two and a half Tribes that led the vanguard of Israel to the Promised Land, and the numerals two and a half are to some extent the badge of their Organisation." This 'two and a half' is the mystical number of the Order, as the Arch Purple lecture explains:

Q. ***"Have you a number?***
A. ***Practical, or mystical.***
Q. ***Mystical?***
A. ***Two, and a half.***
Q. ***What two and a half?***
A. ***The two tribes and a half.***
Q. ***What two tribes and a half?***
A. ***The tribe of Reuben, the tribe of Gad, and the half tribe of Manasseh.***
Q. ***What became of the two tribes and a half?***
A. ***They were restored to their former inheritance on the othe side of Jordan in the land of Gilead***."

Like all secret societies and occult bodies the Royal Arch Purple entrusts its initiates with secret passwords, handshakes, knocks and signs, as keys to open doors into its secret world of mystery. The Royal Arch Purple Order itself owns three permanent passwords.

1. The entrance password for the Arch Purple is: "**Shib-Bo-Leth**."

2. The central password for the Arch Purple is: "**The-Ark-of-God**."

The ignorant candidate is later informed that this mystical password really represents G-O-A-T spelt backwards.

3. The great and grand password for the Arch Purple is: "**The-great-Jehovah-be our-guide**."

A changeable password known as an 'annual password' is made every year and is taken from Scripture in the most superstitious manner. Like all secrets within the Order, this password is given mystically. This is performed by furnishing the membership orally with four numbers. E.g. 2-25-2-12. This would tell the members that the 'annual password' is to be found in the second book of the Bible, Exodus, in the twenty-fifth chapter, in the second verse and is the twelfth word. The password for the year would then be 'offering'. That word, along with the permanent passwords of the Order would then be the members pass into any working Royal Arch Purple Chapter meeting.

The Bible is certainly not a basin to fish superstitious passwords from, but the true, open and infallible revelation of God's Word. The Scriptures say,

"**Now to him that is of power to stablish you according to my gospel, and the preaching of Jesus Christ, according to the revelation of the mystery, which was kept secret since the world began, But now is made manifest, and by the scriptures of the prophets, according to the commandment of the everlasting God, made known to all nations for the obedience of faith**" (Romans 16:25-26).

The Holy Scriptures are the Divine revelation of God, with the intention of showing God's will for man and His plan of salvation. Dealing with Scripture in such a mystical manner can only serve to damage the way in which Royal Arch Purple men look upon God's precious Word and have the ultimate effect of concealing the truths contained therein rather than revealing them. The Bible says, "**Therefore seeing we have this ministry, as we have received mercy, we faint not; But have renounced the hidden things of dishonesty, not walking in craftiness, nor handling the word of God deceitfully; but by manifestation of the truth commending ourselves to every man's conscience in the sight of God. But if our gospel be hid, it is hid to them that are lost: In whom the god of this world hath blinded the minds of them which believe not, lest the light of the glorious gospel of Christ, who is the image of God, should shine unto them**" (2 Corinthians 4:1-4).

Masonic historian C.S.M. Ward explains the significance of passwords, in his Masonic book, '1st Degree Handbook' (p. 37): "*Why passwords at all? Here we wander into a strange field, no less than that of old world magic...such passwords are universal in the great mystery rites, ancient and modern*" ('Hidden Secrets of the Eastern Star' p. 296).

The 'two and a half' is also incorporated into the Order's secret handshake, which identifies one Arch Purple man to another. This is performed by both persons placing pressure with their respective thumbs upon the others middle knuckle thus meeting two and a half finger lengths up the hand, and verifying their Arch Purple membership. This handshake is used when meeting fellow members in both private Chapter meeting and everyday encounters.

The 'two and a half' is used as a mystical knock, to gain admittance to all Royal Arch Purple meetings. In Freemasonry the member wishing entry into the lodge makes three loud knocks, but to achieve the 'two and a half' the Arch Purple make two slow knocks followed by a sharp, quick knock.

The two and a half is used again as the sign of the Arch Purple by coupling the fore finger and middle finger together pointing upward and coupling the small finger and ring finger together downwards and bringing the thumb across in between them. This sign in reality is the same sign as made by the Pope (in the Greek form) when making a statement that he is 'God's representative on earth'.

The Pope's Sign

The secrecy and mysticism surrounding the Royal Arch Purple is in stark contrast to the open ministry and teaching of our beloved Saviour the Lord Jesus Christ. The Lord taught: "**For there is nothing hid, which shall not be manifested; neither was any thing kept secret, but that it should come abroad**" (Mark 4:22).

jacob's ladder

The blindfolded candidate stands nervously in front of the set of steps, known as 'Jacob's ladder'. The initiate is then assisted in climbing up this three stepped ladder (one step at a time), with the help of his guide, whilst the Chaplain reads I Corinthians 13:13. Each rung of the ladder being labelled as he progresses upward, "And now abideth (1) Faith (2) Hope (3) Charity, these three; but the greatest of these is Charity." Unknown to the candidate, at this stage, this climb symbolises one of the great mystical doctrines of all occult bodies.

The Royal Arch Purple, once again, takes this custom directly from Freemasonry where the first-degree Mason is taught: "*The way by which we, as Masons, hope to arrive there* [heaven] *is by the assistance of a ladder, in Scripture called Jacob's ladder. It is composed of many staves or rounds, which point out as many moral virtues, but three principle ones, which are Faith, Hope and Charity: Faith in the Great Architect of the Universe, Hope in salvation, and to be in Charity with all men.*"

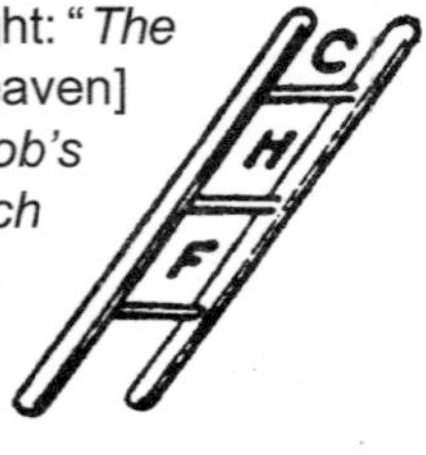

Whilst secret societies surround this peculiar ascent with quasi-biblical language, it is employed, solely, as a means to a deceptive end. This is seen as one carefully examines the teaching of these bodies. The Masonic reference book, 'The Craft and its Symbols' (p. 29) boldly states, "*Freemasons are taught to use the ladder of Jacob to climb towards their reward.*" Here we see one of the core doctrines of all secret societies revealed, that of 'progressive salvation through ritual initiation'.

Masonic adept W.L. Wilmshurst, in his book 'The Meaning of Masonry' (which is addressed to Masons), expounds the spiritual significance of 'Jacob's Ladder', stating: "*Man who has sprung from the earth and developed through the lower kingdoms of nature to his present rational state, has yet to complete his evolution by becoming a god-like being and unifying his consciousness with the Omniscient- to promote which is and has always been the sole aim and purpose of Initiation. To scale this 'height', to attain this expansion of consciousness, is achieved 'by the use of a ladder of many rounds or staves, but of three principle ones, Faith, Hope, and Charity', of which the greatest and most effectual is the last*" (p. 94).

Although labelled Faith, Hope and Charity the steps of this ladder represent the candidate's mystical journey to 'spiritual bliss'. We can see therefore, as the Arch Purple candidate ascends this mysterious ladder, he is taking a blasphemous, symbolic, spiritual journey.

Such a practice is nothing new, but is traced back to the ancient mysteries in which there always existed a peculiar belief in a ladder extending from earth to heaven. Thirty-third degree Freemason Albert Mackey explains: "In all the mysteries of the ancients, we find some allusion to this sacred ladder...Its true origin was lost among the worshippers of the Pagan rites, but the symbol itself, in various modified forms, was retained." Mackey then states that in the mysteries each step was "the representative of a world, or state of existence, through which the soul was supposed to pass in its progress from the first world to the last, or the world of truth" (A Lexicon of Freemasonry, pp. 152-153).

The Royal Arch Purple also attempt to justify this pagan symbol of 'man's progressive salvation', by using the scriptural story where Jacob dreamt of a ladder extending to heaven, as if to justify its use. Then in typically Masonic manner the Arch Purple attempts to Christianise the practice by labelling the steps Faith, Hope and Charity. Scripture makes no reference to Jacob's ladder having three steps and consequently makes no mention of the steps been branded "Faith, Hope and Charity."

The Bible warns, "**For the time will come when they will not endure sound doctrine; but after their own lusts shall they heap to themselves teachers, having itching ears; And they shall turn away their ears from the truth, and shall be turned unto fables**" (2 Timothy 4:3-4).

In the draft to their book, 'History of the Royal Arch Purple Order', the Royal Arch Purple Chapter unashamedly describe the mystical significance and the pagan origins of this practice, although, they conveniently chose to withhold such a passage from their published book. The draft outlines how many organisations use the ladder as "*symbolic of moral, intellectual and spiritual progress*," and explains how, "*The belief in the existence of a ladder leading from earth to heaven was at one time widespread throughout the world. The ancient mythology and religions of the Persians, Scandinavians and Brahmins, used this symbol…In the Mithraic mysteries the seven-runged ladder was a symbol of the ascent of the soul to perfection, each rung being termed as a gate*." No wonder this frank explanation was carefully omitted from the final publication of the Royal Arch Purple Chapter book.

Re-produced by kind permission

The Masonic 'Californian Cipher' (coded ritual) sheds further light on the significance of this practice, by explaining that each step is "emblematic of the three principal stages of human life: Youth, Manhood, and Age." This peculiar Masonic explanation confirms, further, the mystical nature of the ladder.

Significantly, the Royal Arch Purple candidate is also given the same bizarre explanation, albeit it is only given to him in the closing address, long after he has scaled the ladder. He is told: "***You can wear an emblem of the three-stepped ladder representing Faith, Hope, and Charity. By faith we are saved, by hope we are raised, and by charity brought nearer to God. It is also emblematical of the three principal stages in life - Youth, Manhood, and Age***."

The Royal Arch Purple here, like Freemasonry, admits that this ladder is a mystical dualistic symbol, with both physical and spiritual meanings. In keeping with all secret societies they ultimately present the confused candidate with a counterfeit path of salvation. Rather than revealing Christ they hide Him.

Man will always rebel against God's appointed way of entry into heaven. Since the devilishly designed Tower of Babel, man has always thought it possible to climb his way to heaven. The Bible account of Babel says, "And they said, Go to, let us build us a city and a tower, whose top may reach unto heaven; and let us make us a name" (Genesis 11:4). In this instance God destroyed man's abominable counterfeit, as He will every other one constructed. All secret societies by their nature are crude man-made inventions.

Contrary to the teachings of secret societies, Jacob's ladder in Scripture was not literal but symbolic, Jacob having seen it in a dream from God (Genesis 28:12). This ladder is in reality a symbolic Old Testament figure of Christ, the only way by which man can get to heaven.

The truth of God's Word exposes every subtle man-made innovation, however well constructed. Jesus said, "**No man can come to me, except the Father which hath sent me draw him**" (John 6:44).

Clearly no one can climb to Christ - they must be lifted! Man must be drawn God's appointed way. Jesus solemnly outlines in His Word, "**Verily, verily, I say unto you, He that entereth not by the door into the sheepfold, but climbeth up some other way, the same is a thief and a robber. But he that entereth in by the door is the shepherd of the sheep**" (John 10:1-2).

We therefore see that Christ alone is our only way of access to heaven. Jesus said, "**I am the door: by me if any man enter in, he shall be saved, and shall go in and out, and find pasture**" (John 10:9).

coffin

At the top of this ladder, the blindfolded Arch Purple candidate is made to kneel upon a representation of a coffin. The Royal Arch Purple lecturers then outline the importance and profound significance of this solemn act to him: "***With my knees upon a representation of a coffin, my toes extended over the earth, to testify that I was duly prepared to suffer death and all its penalties, before I would divulge anything I had received, or was about to receive.***"

Candidate kneels upon a representation of a coffin
(Drawn by G. Evans)

Here the candidate agrees, by symbolically kneeling upon a representation of a coffin, to suffer the destruction of his own life before he would divulge the bogus teaching of this man-made counterfeit order. Yet Jesus says, "**For the Son of man is not come to destroy men's lives, but to save them**" (Luke 9:56).

How could a believer submit himself to such Arch Purple bondage for what is in reality a counterfeit gospel? This is in stark contrast to Paul the Apostle in Acts 20:24 who was only prepared to pay the ultimate cost, for the Gospel's sake. He said, "**Neither count I my life dear unto myself, so that I might finish my course with joy, and the ministry, which I have received of the Lord Jesus, to testify the gospel of the grace of God**."

And in Philippians 1:17,20-21 he declared: "**I am set for the defence of the gospel... According to my earnest expectation and my hope, that in nothing I shall be ashamed, but that with all boldness, as always, so now also Christ shall be magnified in my body, whether it be by**

life, or by death. For to me to live is Christ, and to die is gain."

The *immediate* source of such a spurious, anti-biblical, Royal Arch Purple custom is (once again) found in the domain of Freemasonry. There, the ignorant candidate is placed upon a representation of a coffin and in some lodges he is even put into an actual wooden one.

The origins and significance of this act are explained in the Masonic dictionary: "In all the ancient mysteries, before an aspirant could claim to participate in the higher secrets of the institution, he was placed within the pastos, or coffin, or in other words was subjected to a solitary confinement for a prescribed period of time, that he might reflect seriously, in seclusion and darkness, on what he was about to undertake, and be reduced to a proper state of mind for the reception of the great and important truths, by a course of fasting and mortification. *This was the symbolical death of the mysteries, and his deliverance from confinement was the act of regeneration, or being born again; or as it was also termed, being raised from the dead.*"

Whilst the three steps of 'Jacob's ladder' represent the three principal stages in life – "Youth, Manhood, and Age." The Arch Purple candidate, by kneeling on this coffin, symbolically indicates he is dying to his old self, and commencing a new mystical life within the Royal Arch Purple Order.

"riding the goat"

After the gravity of his obligation is further impressed upon the Arch Purple candidate the assembled Chapter gather at the back of the steps ('Jacob's ladder') and unfold a large canvas blanket. The blindfolded initiate, who has his back to the blanket is then told to cross his arms whilst still kneeling upon a representation of a coffin.

He is then asked, by the lecturers, "***In whom do you put your trust?***" The nervous candidate answers "***God***" (normally with a little prompting from his guide) whereupon he receives a violent push backward unto the blanket. Here he undergoes one of the most painful and humiliating experiences within the Royal Arch Purple ceremony, when he is brutally kicked and tossed upon the blanket by the assembled Chapter for a number of minutes. This practice is known as "riding the goat."

There is no greater proof of the corrupt nature of the Royal Arch Purple

Order than this demeaning farce. How anyone could interpret it as anything other than an organised disgrace defies belief. One wonders how any Christian could defend such an irreligious sham and explain how it at all promotes holy living or respect for one's fellow man. The Bible solemnly states: "**be ye clean, that bear the vessels of the LORD**" (Isaiah 52:11).

Describing the vulgar practices of the Royal Arch Purple degree in 1878, Thomas Macklin, Grand Secretary of the Grand Orange Lodge of Scotland asserted: "*Viewed in relation to religion not only are they useless but profane and degrading, and ought to restrain the men who practise them from laughing at the mummeries and buffooneries of Popery.*"

Lord Advocate J.B. Balfour attested that on April 27th, 1895, one Rankine of Airblies, Scotland was being initiated into the Arch Purple degree at the Motherwell Orange Lodge when he was blindfolded and tossed so violently in a net or hammock that his spine was dislocated or broken at the neck. He also gave evidence of how in July 1893, one David Blair, while being initiated into the Royal Arch Purple degree at an Orange hall in Belfast, was likewise blindfolded, and while in the act of mounting a table (or ladder) in this condition, fell backwards and was killed.

Such violence within the Order is alluded to in the Chapter's recent book (p. 125). Under the title 'Deterioration in the Arch Purple Discipline' they state "In the early years of the present [20th] century concern was felt by Clerical Brethren and by medical practitioners called upon to render first aid to Arch Purple candidates who had endured a particularly rough travel."

This ceremony, of "riding the goat" is shared by other institutions involved in the mysteries. Former thirty-second degree Mason and Wiccan Witch High Priest, William Schnoebellan testifies to his own experience within Freemasonry: "I was kept in an anteroom. The fellow who was in charge of keeping an eye on me said that I should not worry about riding the goat in the initiation - most guys did it and never fell off. Another fellow came in and said that I shouldn't believe any of 'those stories' about riding the goat. A third fellow winked at me and said they'd only lost a couple of candidates in the last year through death by violence, so I shouldn't worry. It was all done in the manner of good-natured teasing."

Schnoebellan then reveals the foul pagan origins of this blasphemous ceremony, stating: "In the many initiations I observed or actually took part in, I saw a lot of variations of this kind of fraternity house humour. *The only common thing in the many jokes and disturbing allusions was this business about riding the goat. That is interesting when one recalls Albert Pike's teaching about the he-goat of the witches' sabbat, and the way witches in the Middle Ages demonstrated their allegiance to Satan. They had to consent to sexual intercourse with 'the goat'; (usually a high priest rigged up with a goat's head, but occasionally a real demonic form which looked goat-like). Or they had to perform the so-called osculum infamum (obscene kiss) which involved kissing the goat's backside to show their fealty to Satan*" (Beyond The Light p. 87).

The Baphomet
(making the Papal sign denoting the 'hand of God' which is also the 2½)

The 'Romanistic' Knights Templar were known to have introduced such practices into their order after the Crusades had been completed. They were widely accused of practising black magic, blasphemy and homosexuality during their many initiations. Such wickedness was too much even for Rome who began to persecute the Templars. When interrogated the Templars told of strange occultic rituals wherein they worshipped a goat-headed demonic apparition called 'the Baphomet'.

This manifestation, 'the Baphomet', seems to have been regarded with idolatrous reverence amongst the Knights Templar. Some authorities on the subject associate 'the Baphomet' with the Arabic abufihamet, pronounced in Moorish Spanish as bufihmat. This name meaning 'Father of understanding' or 'Father of Wisdom'. The word 'father' in Arabic is taken to imply 'source'. The 'source' in this case being clearly the devil.

Secret societies' obsession with the goat is most striking when one looks at what the Lord says in Scripture: "**When the Son of man shall come in his glory, and all the holy angels with him, then shall he sit upon the throne of his glory: And before him shall be gathered all nations: and he shall separate them one from another, as a shepherd divideth his sheep from the goats: And he shall set the sheep on his right hand, but the goats on the left. Then shall the King say unto them on his right hand, Come, ye blessed of my Father, inherit the kingdom prepared for you from the foundation of the world**" (Matthew 25:31-34).

It is time for the godly to separate from this heathenism!

chapter 7

the consequences of disloyalty

At the end of his "ride on the goat" the candidate is rolled up in a bundle and carried in the canvas or sackcloth sheet to the north-west corner of the Chapter room, where he is informed of the consequences of disloyalty to the Royal Arch Purple. Here the Arch Purple candidate subjects himself to one of the most blasphemous and grossly repulsive forms of bondage imaginable, binding his conscience and spirit, by a devilish blood curse, to this sinful counterfeit body.

Two lecturers converse to explain the penalties as follows: "***Can you explain to me the three great and solemn penalties of a Royal Arch Purpleman?***

First - That I would suffer my throat cut across from ear to ear, my tongue torn out by its roots, and with my body buried in the rough sands of the sea, two and a half cable tow lengths from where the tide ebbs and flows, about twice in a natural day, before I would divulge.

Second - That I would suffer my left breast torn open, my heart and vitals taken therefrom, and with my body given to the vultures of the air, or the wild beasts of the field, as a prey, before I would divulge.

Third and last - That I would suffer no less a penalty than that of having my body severed in two, one part carried east, the other west, taken to the top of some high hill or mountain, the parts thereof burned to ashes, the ashes scattered to the four winds of heaven, so that not a vestige of such a vile or perjured wretch as I should remain amongst men, more especially Royal Arch Purple men, should I divulge, part or parts, secret or sign, sign or token, of anything I had received, or was about to receive, or may hereafter be instructed in, unless to a brother Royal Arch Purpleman, well knowing him to be such, after strict trial and due examination, or upon the word of a well-known brother."

One must ask, how a believer could be part of an Order that confers such evil spiritual bondage upon its members. One wonders what pathetic defence they could give for bestowing such barbaric penalties on the initiate in the light of Holy Writ, or what shred of contrived justification could be uttered to explain how such repugnant rhetoric in any way promotes the Protestant Faith?

The Lord Jesus Christ, in His teaching, revealed the source of such curses when he says, "**The thief** [Satan] **cometh not, but for to steal, and to kill, and to destroy: I am come that they might have life, and that they might have it more abundantly**" (John 10:10).

Clearly, no Christian has the right to bind himself to such wickedness. He is the Lord's unique possession and his body is the temple of the Holy Spirit. The Bible says, "**Know ye not that your body is the temple of the Holy Ghost which is in you, which ye have of God, and ye are not your own? For ye are bought with a price: therefore glorify God in your body, and in your spirit, which are God's**" (1 Corinthians 6:19-20).

The believer is under Divine ownership, being the peculiar possession of the Lord Jesus Christ. He has therefore no right to subject himself to such mutilating curses. 1 Corinthians 3:16-17 says, "**Know ye not that ye are the temple of God, and that the Spirit of God dwelleth in you? If any man defile the temple of God, him shall God destroy; for the temple of God is holy, which temple ye are**."

Like every other word of instruction and every aspect of ceremony within the Royal Arch Purple, the penalties are designed to instil great fear within the candidate, so binding his conscience to the Order. The Bible says, "**There is no fear in love; but perfect love casteth out fear: because fear hath torment. He that feareth is not made perfect in love**" (I John 4:18).

Professing believers within the Royal Arch Purple must repent of this bondage and separate themselves from such sin, renouncing any fear or anxiety that may develop from addressing such a crucial decision. The Bible states, "**For as many as are led by the Spirit of God, they are the sons of God. For ye have not received the spirit of bondage again to fear; but ye have received the Spirit of adoption, whereby we cry, Abba, Father**" (Romans 8:14-15).

The Royal Arch Purple inherited such savage curses directly from the iniquitous pit of Freemasonry, an Order that has always marked its evil influence with this satanic bond. Whilst the Royal Arch Purple places her vulgar penalties into one monstrous abominable concoction, Freemasonry spreads hers over her first three degrees. Nevertheless both orders threaten the same penalties for divulging their teaching and practices.

The obligation of a first degree Freemason (Entered Apprentice degree) says: "Binding myself under no less a penalty than that of having my throat cut across, my tongue torn out by its roots, and buried in the rough sands of the sea at low-water mark, where the tide ebbs and flows twice in twenty four hours, should I ever knowingly or willingly violate this my solemn oath and obligation as an Entered Apprentice Mason. So help me God, and keep me steadfast in the due performance of the same."

The obligation of a second degree Freemason (Fellowcraft degree) says: "Binding myself under no less a penalty than that of having my left breast torn open, my heart plucked out, and given as a prey to the wild beasts of the field and the fowls of the air as a prey."

The obligation of a third degree Freemason (Master Mason degree) says: "Binding myself under no less a penalty than that of having my body severed in two, my bowels taken from thence and burned to ashes, the ashes scattered to the four winds of heaven, so that no more trace or remembrance may be had of so vile and perjured a wretch as I, should I ever knowingly or willingly violate this my solemn obligation as a Master Mason. So help me God, and keep me steadfast in the due performance of the same."

English Freemasonry has been so embarrassed, over recent years, with the public exposure of its wicked curses that it has now omitted these penalties from its Order. The debate started in 1979 when the head of English Masonry, the Duke of Kent, confessed his own "definite sensation of repugnance" over the penalties, and "the distasteful aspect of calling upon God to witness an Oath which is scarcely practical and certainly barbarous." In May 1986 the Masonic Grand Lodge of England reluctantly dropped these penalties, stating they gave "ready material for attack by our enemies and detractors" ('Inside the Brotherhood' p. 64). This decision seemed enforced and was certainly *not* repeated throughout the Masonic world.

As one compares the penalties of the Royal Arch Purple to those of Freemasonry, we see the same vulgar curses and the same common blood bond. Believers must surely see that for a child of God to submit himself to such profane bondage is sin, and sin clearly dishonours Christ. The Bible admonishes the Christian: "**Let your speech be alway with grace, seasoned with salt**" (Colossians 4:6).

The debased language in these curses clearly violates the teaching of Scripture. Ephesians 4:29-30 says, **"Let no corrupt communication proceed out of your mouth, but that which is good to the use of edifying, that it may minister grace unto the hearers. And grieve not the holy Spirit of God, whereby ye are sealed unto the day of redemption**."

The revival preacher Charles G. Finney in his book 'Character and Claims of Freemasonry' alludes to such curses, stating: "The penalty for violating this oath is monstrous, barbarous, savage, and is utterly repugnant to all laws of morality, religion or decency" (p. 35). He then pointedly addresses those involved in such sin: "If they can see no sin in taking and administering such oaths under such penalties, they have succeeded, whether intentionally or not, in rendering themselves utterly blind, as regard the moral character of their conduct...they have put out their own eyes" (p. 59).

No Arch Purple lecturer or administrator involved in this ceremony can shirk his responsibility in imposing these awful curses. He can never argue that they are just mere words. Such barbarous, bloodthirsty language is an anathema to holy living and an offence to a thrice-holy God.

Jesus said "**every idle word that men shall speak, they shall give account thereof in the day of judgement. For by thy words thou shalt be justified, and by thy words thou shalt be condemned** " (Matthew 12:36-37).

Those men who are charged with conferring these penalties are responsible, before God, for placing curses upon many individual lives. James 3:8-10 declares, "**The tongue can no man tame; it is an unruly evil, full of deadly poison. Therewith bless we God, even the Father; and therewith curse we men, which are made after the similitude of God. Out of the same mouth proceedeth blessing and cursing. My brethren, these things ought not so to be**."

Those within the Order who confer such curses must carefully analyse the damage they are inflicting upon others. For those who *profess* the Name of Christ they must reflect upon the obvious spiritual injury they are causing themselves. Separated believers must ask if it is right to have fellowship with such people, since Scripture gives the clear instruction: "**If any man teach otherwise, and consent not to wholesome words, even the words of our Lord Jesus Christ, and to the doctrine which is according to godliness; He is proud, knowing nothing, but doting about questions and strifes of words, whereof cometh envy, strife, railings, evil surmisings, Perverse disputings of men of corrupt minds, and destitute of the truth, supposing that gain is godliness: from such withdraw thyself**" (1 Timothy 6:3-5).

The *true* child of God can have nothing to do with such profane behaviour. I Peter 1:15-16 says, "**But as he which hath called you is holy, so be ye holy in all manner of conversation; because it is written, Be ye holy, for I am holy**."

hot and cold test

As the ceremony continues the Arch Purple candidate receives a cold and hot test. This entails a very cold and a very hot instrument been forced into his chest, this practice is obviously intended to shock the initiate, keeping him in an unsettled state.

This continual unsettling of the nervous candidate is deliberately designed to maintain fear. Evangelical authority on Freemasonry, Tom C McKenney, testifies to his own experience, when initiated into Freemasonry. In his book 'The Deadly Deception' he relates: "I began to experience fear. I couldn't see, didn't know where I was, was half-naked among an unknown number of strangers…I certainly didn't know what would happen next. There was a sense of unreality and helplessness and a rising groundswell of disorientation, insecurity and fear" (p. 22). This experience is one that nearly every Royal Arch Purple man can closely identify with.

Fear is one of the devil's great weapons that he wields against mankind. Fear is his trump card as it struggles with our faith. The believer must say in the words of Scripture: "**The LORD is my light and my salvation; whom shall I fear? the LORD is the strength of my life; of whom shall I be afraid?...Though an host should encamp against me, my heart shall not fear: though war should rise against me, in this will I be confident**" (Psalms 27: 1&3).

Tom C McKenney, reveals the real significance of such a degrading experience in his book 'Please Tell Me', in which he states: "The effect, and its apparent purpose, is humiliation. The candidate is 'reduced to nothing', in this way; he is poor, blind, naked, helpless, confused, and afraid. In addition, he has no idea of where he is, who is watching him, or how many there are. It is a powerful means of subjugation and mind control and may have a permanent detrimental effect on the man, binding him mentally and spiritually to the Lodge and its authority."

It is only at this stage of the ceremony, after being emptied of self, that the Arch Purple candidate is ready to receive.

chapter 8

a mystical enlightenment

Not only does the candidate's mode of dress and ritual participation represent one in darkness seeking light, but the instruction of the Arch Purple Order clearly teaches it.

The Chaplain reads Genesis 1:14-18, where the Scriptures record the creation of the **TWO** *great natural lights* to illuminate the earth, the sun and moon. The sun, the greater light, is to rule the day and, the moon, the lesser light, is to rule the night (V.16). Then without introduction or explanation the Chaplain quotes John 1:5 stating, "And the light shineth in darkness; and the darkness comprehended it not."

No exposition is made of these passages or the context in which they are found, thus placing the light of Lord Jesus Christ, referred to in John 1, in the same context as the natural light provided by the sun and moon. As the ritual progresses, the selective design of these readings become more apparent. Like most of the passages used within secret societies, they are carefully selected to support false practice.

The lecturers then ask the blindfolded candidate: "***What do you stand most in need of?***"

The blindfolded initiate, normally with the assistance of his guide, answers,

"***Light.***" The candidate's blindfold is then removed by the 'Worshipful Master', or some of the brethren present.

This is the most crucial part of the ceremony as it *symbolically* represents the spiritual enlightenment of the initiate. It is at this point that the ceremony reaches its apex. Like all secret society initiates, the Royal Arch Purple candidate has participated in a blasphemous counterfeit travel from darkness to light. This practice is found in all pagan initiations and is designed to represent the core doctrine of all occult bodies, that of 'mystical enlightenment by ritual initiation'.

Like much of the error within the Royal Arch Purple, this teaching comes directly from Freemasonry, where the initiate desires "light" (first degree), "further light" (second degree), and "more light" (third degree). Former thirty-third degree Mason Jim Shaw describes his own initiation into Freemasonry, in his book 'Deadly Deception'. "The Master said to me, 'My brother, in your present blind condition, what do you most desire?'... The Senior Deacon leaned over and whispered in my ear 'Light'...I said, 'Light'. He [the Master] then quoted from Genesis where God said, 'Let there be light' and said, 'In solemn imitation of Him I, in like manner, Masonically declare, let there be light!'... the Senior Deacon ripped off the hoodwink and I was blinded with brilliant light. The Worshipful Master then said, 'And there is light' " (p. 27).

Masonic authority Albert Mackey writes: "*When the candidate makes a demand for light, it is not merely for that material light, which is to remove a physical darkness, that is only the outward form, which conceals the inward symbolism. He craves an intellectual illumination which will dispel the darkness of mental and moral ignorance, and bring to his view, as an eyewitness, the sublime truths of religion, philosophy and science, which it is the great design of Freemasonry to teach... Light, therefore, becomes synonymous with trust and knowledge and darkness with falsehood and ignorance.*"

Christian authority on Freemasonry Tom C. McKenney points out that, "Masonry defines itself as a search for 'light'. This means enlightenment, the acquisition of knowledge that redeems and empowers... This search for the secret knowledge goes on and on, as the individual becomes gradually perfected, redeeming himself!" (Please Tell Me p. 176).

The Royal Arch Purple here aligns itself with all secret societies and Illuminists throughout the world by providing a counterfeit form of light. William T. Still in his evangelical book 'New World Order: - The Ancient Plan of Secret Societies' says: "*All Secret Societies promote an alternative form of enlightenment, an enlightenment which is damning countless souls to hell.*"

It is at this juncture of the ceremony that the Royal Arch Purple lets its deceptive illuministic mask drop, in the most glaring manner imaginable. It is here, at the pinnacle of the ceremony, by the performance of its own counterfeit enlightenment, that the depth of deceit within the Order is fully revealed. It is here, once again, that the rogue Protestant credentials of the Arch Purple Order are graphically exposed.

Daniel says, of Almighty God: "**He revealeth the deep and secret things: he knoweth what is in the darkness, and the light dwelleth with him** " (Daniel 2:22).

The true child of God needs no such mystical enlightenment, as he possesses the blessed light of God's dear Son the Lord Jesus Christ. The Lord Himself declared in John 8:12, "**I am the light of the world, he that followeth me shall not walk in darkness, but shall have the light of life**."

Imagine a professing Christian who has received the true light of the Lord Jesus Christ through salvation, subjecting himself to a ceremony which requires him to divest himself of that light and to conform to the devilishly designed procedures of a man-made sinful institution.

Ephesians 5: 6-11 declares, "**Let no man deceive you with vain words: for because of these things cometh the wrath of God upon the children of disobedience. Be not ye therefore partakers with them. For ye were sometimes darkness, but now are ye light in the Lord: walk as children of light: (For the fruit of the Spirit is in all goodness and righteousness and truth;) Proving what is acceptable unto the Lord. And have no fellowship with the unfruitful works of darkness, but rather reprove them**."

The Arch Purple lecture continues:

Q. ***"Did you get that light?***
A. ***I did.***
Q. ***Who gave it to you?***
A. ***The Worshipful Master, or some of the brethren present."***

Tom C. McKenney reveals the significance of this procedure in his book, 'Please Tell Me' (p. 67): "The blindfold makes the point that the candidate is in complete spiritual darkness and needs the Worshipful Master and the Lodge to bring him out of spiritual darkness and into the light of redemption."

The Psalmist in exalting the Lord says, "**The entrance of thy words giveth light**" (Psalms 119:130).

This blasphemous practice of advancing the 'Worshipful Master' to the position of a 'light bearer' within the Chapter graphically shows the hypocrisy of the 'Master's' place within secret societies. This Arch Purple title (not surprisingly) was inherited from the domain of pagan Masonry. Significantly, the name Lucifer itself means 'light-bearer'. God's precious Word says, "**For Satan himself is transformed into an angel of light. Therefore it is no great thing if his ministers also be transformed as the ministers of righteousness; whose end shall be according to their works**" (2 Corinthians 11:14-15).

Like other similar bodies, the Royal Arch Purple, in typically apostate manner, has presided over the large-scale conferment of the religious titles of 'Worshipful Master', 'Grand Master' and 'Most Worshipful Sovereign Grand Master', upon many ungodly men. The true believer has no authority to countenance, by his membership or his active pronouncements, the profane granting of such *religious titles*. The Lord Himself said of the title Master: "**Neither be ye called masters: for one is your Master, even Christ**" (Matthew 23:10).

William E. Ashbrook in his booklet 'Secretism and Apostasy' (p. 2) writes: "*When men arrogate to themselves such overweening titles they do despite to the Name, which is above every name. They demonstrate afresh that the Satan born delusion 'ye shall be as gods' is still a mighty opiate to deceive those who are untaught in His Word. Herein lie the basic reasons for the fact that all secret orders are basically mutual admiration societies catering first, and always to human vanity.*"

Using the story of the Ark of the Covenant as justification for this counterfeit experience, the Royal Arch Purple Order expound the evil doctrine of mystical enlightenment that is so essential to the very nature of all occult, and secret societies. The lecture teaches:

Q. ***"Where was the resting place of the Ark?***
A. ***In the Tabernacle***
Q. ***How was it adorned?***
A. ***With curtains... of blue, purple, and scarlet, of fine twined linen curiously interwoven with fine needlework.***
Q. ***Of all these colours, which did you choose?***
A. ***Purple***
Q. ***Why purple?***
A. ***Because I received it in darkness, and brought it forth to a marvellous light."***

Such blasphemous teaching violates the infallible truth of God's Word and makes a mockery of the wording of 1 Peter 2: 9, which addresses the blood-bought child of God *alone,* affirming, "**Ye are a chosen generation, a royal priesthood, an holy nation, a peculiar people; that ye should shew forth the praises of him who hath called you out of darkness into his marvellous light**."

The Scriptures here show how the child of God has been removed from the world of darkness and placed into the jurisdiction of Christ's marvellous light.

The Bible also says, "**Giving thanks unto the Father, which hath made us meet to be partakers of the inheritance of the saints in light: Who hath delivered us from the power of darkness, and hath translated us into the kingdom of his dear Son: In whom we have redemption through his blood, even the forgiveness of sins**" (Colossians 1:12-14).

No man, whether Protestant or Roman Catholic, red, yellow, black or white will ever enter into *true* enlightenment, but by the Lord Jesus Christ and his shed blood on Calvary. Brother in the Lord, within the Royal Arch Purple, how can you defend such blasphemy? Scripture solemnly warns: "**Woe unto them that call evil good, and good evil; that put darkness for**

light, and light for darkness" (Isaiah 5:20). Every believer within the Royal Arch Purple Order is clearly, by his very membership, condoning apostasy.

intimidation

Immediately after the blindfold is removed the Arch Purple candidate is faced with the most shocking of sights, when three of the brethren solemnly stand pointing dangerous weapons at him. The lecturers then explain the significance of such an intimidating sight. This is again outlined in catechism form.

Q. "What did you first behold?
A. Death in all its horrors, staring me in the face, a spear to pierce my heart, a sword to run me through, and a gun to shoot me, should I divulge."

Many Chapters use real guns to impress the grave consequence of betraying the Order. This custom has often involved the firing of a blank round at the candidate to further instil fear in to him, thus securing rigid loyalty to the Institution. This dangerous practice has resulted in tragedy over the years.

Tony Gray in his book 'The Orange Order' (p. 211) mentions to one such incident when discussing the Arch Purple degree. He refers to the Contemporary Review for August 1896, which explains how "a candidate for the Orange Order was shot dead at his initiation; he was killed by a bullet from a revolver used in some form of 'Russian roulette' ceremony!"

The Royal Arch Purple Chapter's book (p. 160) refers to another fatality in the early 1900's, when one of its members, Samuel Tweedie of Newry, was charged with causing the death of a candidate in that town by a pistol wound.

This incident was exposed by the Protestant Truth Society in its pamphlet condemning the Arch Purple in 1925. They revealed: "It appears that Tweedie was unaware that the pistol used in the ceremony was loaded with other than blank cartridge. The jury acquitted him of culpable homicide under the circumstances."

This practice, however beautifully packaged, is a sinister act carefully designed to instil great fear within the candidate. It is also designed to secure secrecy, and is the foundation upon which all secret societies are built, and exist. It is difficult to see how a truly saved man could condone such evil. This custom is certainly not biblical. God's Word again states, "**God hath not given us the spirit of fear; but of power, and of love, and of a sound mind**" (2 Timothy 1:7).

Satan, the 'deceiver' has enticed many evangelical men into the Royal Arch Purple, and unbeknown to themselves, once within, he has dulled their spiritual senses through the sinful imposition of fear. Many brethren, even when leaving the Institution, testify to a great sense of fear surrounding them. The Bible reveals that, "**The fear of man bringeth a snare: but whoso putteth his trust in the LORD shall be safe**" (Proverbs 29:25).

The child of God does not have to fear man, a sinful institution or any of its penalties. His trust is in God alone to preserve his feeble life. How often our forefathers took solace in the precious words of the Lord Jesus Christ: "**Fear not them which kill the body, but are not able to kill the soul: but rather fear him which is able to destroy both soul and body in hell**" (Matthew 10:28).

three great lights

The candidate is then faced with a mystical three-branched candlestick flickering before his eyes. He is told that it represents 'the three great lights'.

The Arch Purple lecture explains its meaning.

Q. ***"What did you next behold?***
A. ***Three great lights in the east.***
Q. ***What did these three great Lights represent?***
A. ***Spiritually, Father, Son and Holy Ghost, co-equal and co-eternal; but carnally, the Sun, Moon and Stars, and the Worshipful Master.***

Q. Why the Sun, Moon and Stars, and the Worshipful Master?
A. First - The Sun, the greater light, to rule the day. Second - The Moon and Stars, the lesser lights, to rule the night. Third - The Worshipful Master standing in the midst with a drawn sword in his hand. He also carried the Bible, and the book of rules and regulations, and the seal of the Chapter placed thereon. The Bible to be the rule and guide of his faith and practice. The book of rules and regulations to enable him to rule and govern his Royal Arch Purple Chapter, or, in his unavoidable absence, cause the same to be done by some fit and qualified brother. The seal teaches me that should I receive a summons or document whereon that seal is legally affixed, I am in duty bound to attend thereto, as well as to keep the secrets of my Royal Arch Purple brethren within my breast, as well as my own, murder and treason excepted."
Here as the initiation nears its end the candidate is again reminded of his grave obligation of allegiance to his brethren.

The superstitious use of burning candles is here employed to further impress upon the candidate the deep spiritual significance of his 'mystical enlightenment'. It is nevertheless ironic that one of the most immediate practices purged from the Church at the Reformation was the widespread use of burning candles. It is amazing to see how such a pagan custom has worked its way into a so-called Protestant order.

Masonic author Bernard E. Jones, who wrote the 'Freemasons' Guide and Compendium', states, "The burning of candles in holy places seems to have been a heathen idea originally, and there was great opposition to it in the Early Christian Church" (p. 359).

Furthermore, the teaching that accompanies this superstitious practice involves both an attack upon the Godhead and also the infallibility of God's Holy Word. The Royal Arch Purple here blasphemously throws the blessed Trinity into an unholy alliance with the sun, moon and stars, and the 'Worshipful Master'. (Such profanity!) It is only at this juncture that the full significance of the Order's (earlier) coupling of Genesis 1:14-18 with John 1:5 is understood.

The Royal Arch Purple lecture explains that these 'three great lights' have a dualistic meaning. ***Spiritually,*** *they* represent "Father, Son and Holy Ghost, co-equal and co- eternal; but ***carnally***, the Sun, Moon and Stars, and the Worshipful Master." In its recent book, the Chapter state that they represent the "Greater Lights" and "lesser lights," respectively.

This Arch Purple teaching is again seen to have NO biblical foundation! Scripture speaks of only *two great lights*, the sun and the moon, which were created to provide natural light to the earth. Genesis 1:16 says: "**And God made two great lights; the greater light to rule the day, and the lesser light to rule the night: he made the stars also**."

In order to dispel any doubts, that this dualistic symbol is anything other than heathenish, the Arch Purple candidate is informed that 'the three great lights' are to be found *"in the east."* In Ezekiel 8 we see God exposing the same type of idolatry which the children of Israel had brought into the house of God. Ironically, they too performed their error in *secret*. The Lord spoke through His prophet Ezekiel: "**hast thou seen what the ancients of the house of Israel do in the dark** [or obscurity], **every man in the chambers of his imagery**?" (V.12).

The prophet Ezekiel continues, "**And he brought me into the inner court of the LORD's house, and, behold, at the door of the temple of the LORD, between the porch and the altar, were about five and twenty men, with their backs toward the temple of the LORD, and their faces toward the east; and they worshipped the sun toward the east**" (V.16).

The Lord's response is chilling, when we think of the state of our beloved Province. He says: "**Is it a light thing to the house of Judah that they commit the abominations which they commit here? for they have filled the land with violence, and have returned to provoke me to anger: and, lo, they put the branch to their nose. Therefore will I also deal in fury: mine eye shall not spare, neither will I have pity: and though they cry in mine ears with a loud voice, yet will I not hear them**" (Ezekiel 8:17-18).

The Royal Arch Purple Order refers to 'the three great lights' in its closing address. When referring to the subject of 'death' they state, "*this is not the end of man, nor the glorious aspirations of the brethren of our Order, who, true to their principles, look for the manifestations of* ***the three great lights in the east****, representing Death, Resurrection, and Ascension; and bid us turn our eyes with faith and confidence beyond the silent grave towards the dawn of a glorious eternity*." Here again we see the rogue nature of the Royal Arch Purple exposed. They amazingly point the bewildered candidate to a three-branched, dualistic, heathenish candlestick in the east for their hope of salvation.

This heretical teaching undermines the authority and supremacy of Scripture, which assures the child of God that he is in the hands of his Great High Priest, the Lord Jesus Christ. The Bible says that the true believer is "**Looking for that blessed hope, and the glorious appearing of the great God and our Saviour Jesus Christ; Who gave himself for us, that he might redeem us from all iniquity, and purify unto himself a peculiar people, zealous of good works**" (Titus 2:13-14).

In their book, 'History of the Royal Arch Purple Order' (p. 197), the Arch Purple Chapter deceitfully tell its readership that the three lesser lights represent, "the Sun, Moon and Stars." Nevertheless when one studies the internal teaching of the Order we learn that the three lesser lights really represent "the Sun, Moon and Stars, *and the Worshipful Master.*"

After tampering with the truth about the inner components of the lesser lights, the Arch Purple Chapter explain how they "represent the carnal or physical light" thus placing the 'Worshipful Master' in the same realm as the sun, moon and stars, as a 'light bearer'.

This extra-biblical teaching is condemned in Deuteronomy 4:2, which declares: "**Ye shall not add unto the word which I command you, neither shall ye diminish ought from it, that ye may keep the commandments of the LORD your God which I command you**."

The sun, moon and stars, known in Scripture as the 'the host of heaven', have always been the focus of heathen Baal worship throughout time. Even the children of Israel turned towards this idolatry at particular times of great compromise. Interestingly, such error was always performed behind a veil of great secrecy.

Under the evil reign of King Ahaz we learn that, "**the children of Israel did secretly those things that were not right against the LORD their God**," and Scripture continues, "**they followed vanity, and became vain, and went after the heathen that were round about them, concerning whom the LORD had charged them, that they should not do like them. And they left all the commandments of the LORD their God, and made them molten images, even two calves, and made a grove, and worshipped all the host of heaven, and served Baal**" (II Kings 17:9, 15-16).

When Israel enjoyed a godly King, he normally distanced the nation from all appearance of Baal worship. II Kings 23:4 records how King Josiah commanded the priests to "**bring forth out of the temple of the LORD all the vessels that were made for Baal, and for the grove, and for all the host of heaven: and he burned them without Jerusalem in the fields of Kidron, and carried the ashes of them unto Bethel** ."

Surely the time has come in our history to do the same and return to the old trusted paths. The Bible commands us to: "**Prove all things; hold fast that which is good. Abstain from all appearance of evil** " (1Thessalonians 5:21-22).

The idolatrous teaching of the Royal Arch Purple has clearly originated from that child of the mysteries, Freemasonry, and is an affront to the name of Protestantism. Former thirty-third degree Freemason Jim Shaw, (in relating his own experience) confirms the immediate source of this teaching on the three great lights. In his evangelical book, 'The Deadly Deception' p. 27, after explaining the greater lights as, the Bible, square and compass, he states that the 'Worshipful Master' "referred to the three candles around the altar and said they represent the three lesser lights of Freemasonry, which in reality are the sun, the moon, and the Worshipful Master of the Lodge."

The Arch Purple Chapter's book (p. 197) explains how the lesser lights (the sun, moon and stars, and the 'Worshipful Master'), are provided to "*assist us in our daily lives.*" Then, obviously feeling the need to exonerate themselves, they endeavour to argue that the lesser lights are "not subjects of adoration in their own right" (How helpful!).

The only light-bearer needed to "assist us in our daily lives" is the Lord Jesus Christ. In fact the Bible condemns the bestowing of such a blasphemous title of 'Worshipful Master' upon any other man. In Matthew 23 the Lord rebukes both the *religious title* of 'Father' which is so commonly used by Rome, and the *religious title* of 'Master' which is used by all secret societies.

Jesus says: "**And call no man your father upon the earth: for one is your Father, which is in heaven. Neither be ye called masters: for one is your Master, even Christ**" (V. 9-10).

Once again, the Royal Arch Purple (like all secret societies) place the 'Worshipful Master' in the position of a 'light-bearer'. This exaltation of a mere mortal reveals the true heathenish nature and hypocrisy of the 'Master's' position within the Chapter. The 'Worshipful Master', who actually sits in the east in Freemasonry, is symbolically the human embodiment of the sun. His deputy, the Senior Warden, who sits in the west, represents the moon. Masonic adept W.L. Wilmshurst touches this matter in his book 'The Meaning of Masonry', where he expounds, in great detail, the esoteric (or hidden) spiritual significance of this peculiar custom. He states that "The Senior Warden, whilst the Master's chief executive officer, is his antithesis and opposite pole...At best he in the West can but reflect and transmit that greater light from the East, as the moon receives and reflects sunlight" (pp. 101-102).

Even the Royal Arch Purple Chapter seems uneasy with this whole subject of the three greater and lesser lights. In the Chapter's published book, they hesitantly ask, "Could this have been part of the objections raised by the Lifford brethren in 1813 when they complained of the heathenish rites?"

In establishing the answer to the Royal Arch Purple Chapter's question we must carefully explore the annals of history. We discover in Orangeism's archive material that Lifford Orange District was in fact commenting on the *whole* Arch Purple ceremony rather than one individual act within it. Like nearly all the Orange family throughout the 1800s, Lifford Orange brethren strongly opposed the heathenish practices of the Royal Arch Purple. When they heard of the degrading Royal Arch Purple degree being secretly worked in parts of Ireland they wrote to the Grand Orange Lodge of Ireland on 16th January 1813 to expose such false practices.

Lifford testified: "Several Lodges introduce the man to be made, naked and hoodwinked, and go through a long and tedious form, and then he has to take an obligation, in many respects different from that prescribed by the Regulations of the Grand Lodge, at another time a man is entered and has to pass through several forms, and perform several other things, and take another oath."

The Grand Lodge of Ireland, which opposed this indecent ceremony from its inception in 1798 to the early 20th century responded promptly to Lifford's concerns on 27th January 1813. In a strongly worded statement, they declared: "*your Memorial containing an account of the Heathenish and indecent ceremonies practised themselves by some calling themselves Orangemen, I laid before the Grand Lodge of Ireland, who heard it read with the most poignant grief and indignation: and I am directed to say, that nothing can be more contrary to our Loyal Institution than such practices. The Principles of the Orange Institution, following the Principles of the Christian Religion, are precise, clear, and simple, easily understood, and easily practised; Piety towards God - Loyalty towards our King, and Good Will to all our Neighbours - To enter into Societies professing and practising these Principles, requires no idle or ridiculous ceremony... we have no mystery, or superstitious Rites; For we well know, where mystery begins, honesty terminates...Entreat them to put away from them Practices which they have adopted so derogatory to our Glorious Institution - tell them these were the very Practices and Ceremonies of the Illuminati of France and Germany, who brought their country to slavery and ruin. Ask them how such Practices can conduce to the Maintenance of the Protestant cause, to the advancement of Loyalty, or the Good of the People?*" How times have changed!

chapter 9

a false hope

The Royal Arch Purple Chapter hypocritically address the topic of 'the three great lights', in their recent book. In one breath they affirm that "true light can only be found in the Trinity." In the next breath they amazingly declare that "***everyday living will and can be enhanced by the help of those in the chain of fellowship who had received that Purple in the darkness of ignorance and brought it to the true light of understanding***" (p. 193).

Masonic authority Albert Mackey pronounced that, "*Darkness among Freemasons is emblematical of ignorance... the absence of light must be the absence of knowledge... In the spurious Freemasonry of the ancient mysteries, the aspirant was always shrouded in darkness, as a preparatory step to the reception of the full light of knowledge*" (A Lexicon of Freemasonry p. 68).

The Royal Arch Purple Chapter makes a subtle point of highlighting the fact that the '*chain of fellowship*' described, includes only those that have "received that Purple in the darkness of ignorance and brought it to the true light of understanding." The Chapter then elevates this fake '*chain of fellowship*' as the great hope to enhance men's "everyday living." Nevertheless Jesus said, "**I will build *my church*; and the gates of hell shall not prevail against *it***" (Matthew 16:18).

This Arch Purple structure is carefully devised to draw men away from the only chain of fellowship that God accepts, the Church, towards a proud, arrogant, largely unregenerate institution. The believer has no need to undermine his privileged position within the body of believers by joining such an unscriptural invention. Jeremiah 17:5 says, "**Thus saith the LORD; Cursed be the man that trusteth in man, and maketh flesh his arm**."

In their recent publication (p. 192) the Royal Arch Purple Chapter repeats its sinful elitist attitude, stating, **"**It should always be stressed that *we not only put our trust in God but we should all cultivate trust in our fellow men, **especially those within the Institution***." Such instruction blatantly violates the teaching of Scripture.

Psalms 40:4 says, "**Blessed is that man that maketh the LORD his trust, and respecteth not the proud**." Whilst the Arch Purple tells its members, "we should all cultivate trust in our fellow men, especially those within the Institution," the Bible directs the child of God: **"As we have therefore opportunity, let us do good unto all men, especially unto them who are of the household of faith"** (Galatians 6:10). Constantly throughout this degree the Royal Arch Purple is found mimicking Scripture. This is a practice that runs contrary to the principles of Protestantism and is more akin to Roman Catholicism.

Christian within the Royal Arch Purple, which body enjoys your ultimate allegiance and commitment? Where does your heart really lie? Clearly you *cannot* meet the demands of both bodies!

The Royal Arch Purple book (p.192) further teaches: "*Only by showing trust in God* **and** *cultivating trust in our fellows can we hope to elevate our lives to a higher plane and so lead to a happier and fuller life.*" Here again the Order deceptively couples trusting our fellow man with trusting God as necessary to "elevating our lives to a higher plane and so lead to a happier and fuller life."

One does not need to be a theologian to realise such error cannot be found anywhere in Holy Writ. The Bible declares in that famous passage which set off the Lewis Revival: "**Who shall ascend into the hill of the LORD? or who shall stand in his holy place? He that hath clean hands, and a pure heart; who hath not lifted up his soul unto vanity, nor sworn deceitfully. He shall receive the blessing from the LORD, and righteousness from the God of his salvation**" (Psalms 24:3-5).

Such absurd teaching and arrogant elitism which has ensnared many believers within the Royal Arch Purple, must be completely purged out of the evangelical camp lest a "little leaven leaveneth the whole lump" (1 Corinthians 5:6). Christians within the Arch Purple are clearly dividing their ultimate loyalty to God and His people, with a man-made sinful counterfeit.

the key of the ark

The Royal Arch Purple addresses the subject of the 'Ark of the Covenant' in its initiation. And in keeping with the whole ceremony they do so in the most mysterious manner possible. Teaching in catechism form, the lecturers repeat this dialogue:

Q. ***"Have you the central password?***
A. ***I have***
Q. ***Will you give it to me?***
A. ***I will, if you begin. The - Ark - of - God...***
Q. ***Have you the key of the Ark?***
A. ***I have.***
Q. ***Where do you keep it?***
A. ***In a little double-rowed ivory box, more precious to me than gold or silver.***
Q. ***Will you give it to me?***
A. ***No.***
Q. ***Will you lend it to me?***
A. ***No.***
Q. ***Will you sell it to me?***
A. ***No."***

The source and true meaning of this teaching is not apparent, but what is significant is where it isn't found. Nowhere in Holy Writ does one find any instruction about the 'Ark of the Covenant' having a key, nor do we find the contents of this catechism *anywhere* in Scripture.

This teaching, like most within the Arch Purple is extra-biblical and is designed to support esoteric (occult) teaching. The Bible solemnly says: **"To the law and to the testimony: if they speak not according to this word, it is because there is no light in them**" (Isaiah 8:20).

a false assurance

The Royal Arch Purple ceremony nears its end with a closing address on the symbols of the Order. After alluding to the Bible and other symbols (explaining their importance), they close in an erroneous manner by presenting a false gospel, with a solemn address on the subject of death. The Arch Purple here sanction the use of the 'coffin symbol', to the newly initiated candidate, as an ominous reminder of his weighty responsibility to the Order.

The address states that, "***You can wear an emblem of the coffin, a representation of which you knelt upon, to take that part of your solemn obligation. It reminds us of death, which may come to everyone, break the brittle thread of life, and launch us into eternity. At this very moment the Angel of death has received the awful mandate to strike many of our brethren from the roll of human existence. If perchance we have escaped the numerous evils incident to childhood, and youth, and with health and vigour have arrived at manhood, yet and withal we too shall be cut off and gathered to the land where our fathers have gone before us***."

Furthermore, it continues, "***Whilst reflecting upon the solemn thought of death, this degree teaches us that all must die; we follow our brethren to the brink of the grave, and, standing on the shores of a vast ocean, we gaze with exquisite anxiety until the last struggle is o'er. We see them sink into its fathomless abyss, and feel our own feet sliding from the precarious brink on which we stand. A few more suns, and we too shall be whelmed neath death's awful wave to rest in the stilly shades, where darkness and silence shall for ever reign, around our melancholy abode***."

The *true* child of God does not share this awful dread of death, which the Royal Arch Purple so poetically describes. His hope is summed up in (the beloved) Psalms 23:4, "**Yea, though I walk through the valley of the shadow of death, I will fear no evil: for thou art with me; thy rod and thy staff they comfort me**." One wonders whether this confusing Arch Purple address disguises the false doctrine of soul sleep?

The address comes to a close, in typically neo-Masonic manner: "***But this is not the end of man, nor the glorious aspirations of the brethren of our Order, who, true to their principles, look for the manifestations of the three great lights in the east, representing Death, Resurrection, and Ascension. And bid us turn our eyes with faith and confidence beyond the silent grave towards the dawn of a glorious eternity***."

Then, as if to mimic Scripture they conclude, "***Finally my brethren, by the careful regulation of our lives, pondering well our words, and the cultivation of brotherly love and loyalty, we may obtain our Great Grand Master's approbation*** [authorisation and approval]. ***Then, when the embers of mortality are faintly glimmering in the sockets of existence, and death does come, and we are ushered into the Grand Lodge above, there shall be revealed to us the real secrets of the Ark of God; and we shall realise, for all eternity that the Great Jehovah has been our Guide***."

Here, at the conclusion of this offensive ceremony we see an abhorrent, counterfeit gospel expounded. In common with all secret societies, the Royal Arch Purple presents a false hope of salvation through an upright character and good works. Nevertheless, the Bible says: "**For by grace are ye saved through faith; and that not of yourselves: it is the gift of God: Not of works, lest any man should boast**" (Ephesians 2:8-9).

Nowhere in this closing address do we hear the Name of our beloved Saviour the Lord Jesus Christ mentioned, nor do we learn of His great atoning death on Calvary. As in Freemasonry, the Royal Arch Purple has an invented substitute called the "Great Grand Master." This is a title, which Scripture does not allow, and is clearly unwarranted. The Bible declares: "**Neither is there salvation in any other: for there is none other name under heaven given among men, whereby we must be saved**" (Acts 4:12).

Satan clearly knows there is power in the Name of the Lord Jesus Christ, for it is in Christ alone that we find salvation and in His precious Name that we have victory. Philippians 2:9-11 says, "**Wherefore God also hath highly exalted him, and given him a name which is above every name: That at the name of Jesus every knee should bow, of things in heaven, and things in earth, and things under the earth; And that every tongue should confess that Jesus Christ is Lord, to the glory of God the Father**."

Well could the General Assembly of the Presbyterian Church in Ireland ask, in a text passed in recent years condemning Freemasonry: "Can a Christian be content with definitions of God which fall short of the Biblical revelation of God's character?" Friend, a gospel without Christ is 'another gospel'.

The Royal Arch Purple makes much in its address about the moral righteousness of its members without emphasising the biblical truth that such conduct will never render a man justified in the eyes of God. The Order expounds such teaching by conveniently ignoring the blight, which contaminates every man – ***sin***. Sin entered the world in the Garden of Eden when Adam fell. The Bible says, "**Wherefore, as by one man sin entered into the world, and death by sin; and so death passed upon all men, for that *all have sinned***" (Romans 5:12). Everyone since Adam has inherited his sinful nature. The Psalmist outlines this grim reality: "**Behold, I was shapen in iniquity; and in sin did my mother conceive me**" (Psalms 51:5). It is this corrupt nature that ultimately separates man from God.

Regardless of how man sees himself or what grandiose titles he bestows upon himself, he is still a vile sinner in need of redemption. The Bible says that we are all "**by nature the children of wrath**" (Ephesians 2:3).

Salvation does not come through a ritual or obedience to a set of secret society rules invented by man. Salvation does not even come through being an upright person. The Bible says, "**We are all as an unclean thing, and all our righteousnesses are as filthy rags**" (Isaiah 64:6). Man's own garments are clearly stained by sin. Accepting one's sinful condition means looking to God's *only* provision for lost sinners, namely His impeccable sinless Son, the Lord Jesus Christ.

The Bible says, "**For if by one man's offence death reigned by one; much more they which receive abundance of grace and of the gift of righteousness shall reign in life by one, Jesus Christ. Therefore as by the offence of one judgment came upon all men to condemnation; even so by the righteousness of one the free gift came upon all men unto justification of life. For as by one man's disobedience many were made sinners, so by the obedience of one shall many be made righteous. Moreover the law entered, that the offence might abound. But where sin abounded, grace did much more**" (Romans 5:17-20).

The Lord Jesus Christ (the spotless Lamb of God) voluntarily laid down His life for lost, hell-deserving sinners. The Bible says, "**And all things are of God, who hath reconciled us to himself by Jesus Christ, and hath given to us the ministry of reconciliation... For he hath made him to be sin for us, who knew no sin; that we might be made the righteousness of God in him**" (2 Corinthians 5:18&21).

The way by which God pardons a man's sin, is through the shedding of blood. The Bible clearly says, "**without shedding of blood is no remission**" (Hebrews 9:22).

Christ paid the believers' penalty in full by His vicarious atoning death, thus relieving him fully of his guilt, and purchasing his complete redemption. 1 Peter 1:18-19 says, "**Forasmuch as ye know that ye were not redeemed with corruptible things, as silver and gold, from your vain conversation received by tradition from your fathers; But with the precious blood of Christ, as of a lamb without blemish and without spot.**"

Like all secret societies, the Royal Arch Purple address carefully omits any mention of the blood of the Lord Jesus Christ. For a so-called Protestant Order to omit the blood from the Gospel is to propagate a false gospel. The Bible admonishes us, "**If we say that we have fellowship with him, and walk in darkness, we lie, and do not the truth: But if we walk in the light, as he is in the light, we have fellowship one with another, and the blood of Jesus Christ his Son cleanseth us from all sin**" (I John 1:6-7).

The *true* believer can joyfully sing with the hymn writer:

"What can wash away my stain?
Nothing but the blood of Jesus,
What can make me whole again?
Nothing but the blood of Jesus."

Ephesians 2:13 states: "**But now in Christ Jesus ye who sometimes were far off are made nigh by the blood of Christ.**" Every true child of God should flee the very ground of this deceptive Arch Purple counterfeit.

We also find the bold assumption, throughout this whole initiation, that all Arch Purple brethren go to heaven whilst ignoring the clear scriptural requirements of true faith and repentance. The Bible says: "**That if thou shalt confess with thy mouth the Lord Jesus, and shalt believe in thine heart that God hath raised him from the dead, thou shalt be saved. For with the heart man believeth unto righteousness; and with the mouth confession is made unto salvation**" (Romans 10:9-10).

Every sinner, whether an Arch Purple man or not, must come to the Lord Jesus Christ in faith with a repentant heart. The Lord Himself said: "**Except ye repent, ye shall all likewise perish**" (Luke 13:3).

Secret societies by their nature are cunningly designed to lure men away from God rather than to Him. Subtly embodied within every aspect of Arch Purple practice and doctrine is deceitful error. They sinfully point their initiates to an institution with its obligatory demands of loyalty to its own membership, as opposed to God ordained earthly relationships. This kind of arrogant teaching within the Royal Arch Purple leads its members to believe that acceptance of its forms and rituals guarantees eternal life.

The roots of such error, like every aspect of Arch Purple teaching, can be found in pagan Masonry. Freemasons receive the same false hope, when they are told, in the third degree, that "when we shall be summoned from this sublunary abode, we may ascend to the *Grand Lodge above*, where the world's great Architect lives and reigns for ever" (Masonic Manual p. 73).

The 'Grand Lodge above' which secret societies so consistently refer to, is clearly not the heaven of the Bible. It is a fabricated alternative abode where secret society members are promised to ascend to, without trusting in Christ.

The true believer, who comes God's ordained way, can rest with deep assurance on the words of Christ: "**In my Father's house are many mansions: if it were not so, I would have told you. I go to prepare a place for you. And if I go and prepare a place for you, I will come again, and receive you unto myself; that where I am, there ye may be also**" (John 14:2-3).

While the Royal Arch Purple remind their initiates of the certainty of death, they carefully omit to warn them of the solemn appointment which all shall meet after death, that of the judgement. Hebrews 9:27 says, "**it is**

appointed unto men once to die, but after this the judgment." It is here that true justice will finally be exercised. 2 Corinthians 5:10 says, "**For we must all appear before the judgment seat of Christ; that every one may receive the things done in his body, according to that he hath done, whether it be good or bad.**"

While the Royal Arch Purple draws the attention of its candidates to the important matter of eternity, in this closing discourse, it is exclusively in the context of a heavenly reward for its brethren. By doing so, they make the unacceptable assumption that *every* Royal Arch Purple man is destined for heaven and eternal bliss without warning them of the grim reality of hell for all those who die outside of Christ. In fact the Order avoids the solemn subject of hell altogether.

Whilst the Royal Arch Purple Order is evasive on the doctrine of hell, the Lord is clearly not. Revelation 21:7-8 declares, "**He that overcometh shall inherit all things; and I will be his God, and he shall be my son. But the fearful, and unbelieving, and the abominable, and murderers, and whoremongers, and sorcerers, and idolaters, and all liars, shall have their part in the lake which burneth with fire and brimstone: which is the second death.**"

Evangelist John R. Rice in his book 'Lodges Examined By The Bible' (p. 54) declares: "Beyond any shadow of a doubt, then, the lodges deny the gospel of Jesus Christ. They are blind leaders of the blind, leading millions of men and women away from salvation by the blood. They lead them to depend upon their own righteousness and doubtless lead them to feel no need of regeneration, lead them to ignore the warnings of the gospel, and so lead them to fall at last unprepared into a devil's Hell!"

The Lord encountered the same proponents of dead religion in his day, when he confronted the 'religious' Pharisees of the day. In doing so, He directly addressed the solemn subject of hell, saying, "**Woe unto you, scribes and Pharisees, hypocrites! for ye are like unto whited sepulchres, which indeed appear beautiful outward, but are within full of dead men's bones, and of all uncleanness."** He then asserted, "**Ye serpents, ye generation of vipers, how can ye escape the damnation of hell**?" (Matthew 23: 27&33).

In proclaiming a self-righteous gospel, as the Royal Arch Purple clearly does, they are leading countless souls to a Christless eternity. Iain H.

Murray once cautioned, "Error, preached as truth, has contributed to the delusion of multitudes who are lost." Christians who belong to the Royal Arch Purple Order, are countenancing, by their continued membership, a false hope of salvation for the unsaved. How sobering are the words of Scripture, "**I marvel that ye are so soon removed from him that called you into the grace of Christ unto another gospel: Which is not another; but there be some that trouble you, and would pervert the gospel of Christ. But though we, or an angel from heaven, preach any other gospel unto you than that which we have preached unto you, let him be accursed**" (Galatians 1:6-8).

This ambiguous Royal Arch Purple concoction, like every other counterfeit emanating from hell, is ultimately designed to direct men away from God's only provision for lost sinners, the Lord Jesus Christ. Such a deceptive address, not surprisingly, leaves the candidate in a horrible state of confusion and leads him away from the simplicity of the true biblical faith. The Bible instructs the believer to "**Preach the word; be instant in season, out of season; reprove, rebuke, exhort with all longsuffering and doctrine. For the time will come when they will not endure sound doctrine; but after their own lusts shall they heap to themselves teachers, having itching ears; And they shall turn away their ears from the truth, and shall be turned unto fables**" (2 Timothy 4:2-4).

Jesus calls His people out of error. He says, "**And ye shall know the truth, and the truth shall make you free**" (John 8:32). Which gospel do we choose?

chapter 10

symbolism

One of the most prominent, and yet deceptive, aspects of the Royal Arch Purple is its symbolism. This imagery, like the teaching and practices of the Order, was inherited directly from Freemasonry and is universally recognised. Its true significance is disguised beneath a thick veil of secrecy, mystery and deception; nevertheless, as we analyse the mystical nature of the symbolism employed within the Royal Arch Purple it is not difficult to recognise its occult origins.

Freemasonry itself, which is widely accepted as the largest and most influential occult body existing throughout the world today, inherited its imagery, known as esoteric (or occult) symbolism, directly from the fountainhead of the pagan ancient mysteries. Evangelical author of 'Christ the Christian and Freemasonry', and himself an Ulsterman, W.J. McK. McCormick states, "Whatever rite or symbol we examine in Masonry, in spite of protests well-meaning or otherwise, from those who have been deceived, we find that it derives its true origin and meaning from the Ancient Mysteries" (p. 94).

All occult symbolism is in fact *dualistic* in meaning or interpretation, in that, it has an exoteric or outward meaning (known to the masses) and an esoteric or hidden meaning (known only to the elect few). Occultist Fredrick Goodman in his book 'Magical Symbols' (p. 6) explains: *The true magic symbol is an image which hides an inner meaning. This meaning is usually cunningly hidden behind a form which most people think they can understand immediately*."

He further states that, "True magical symbols are 'disguises' for ideas, how their forms are so arranged as to provide a clue to some hidden meaning. The 'hidden meanings' are often very subtle, and an ability to recognise magical symbols must be developed by anyone who wishes to seek these out" (p. 11).

Christian authority on Freemasonry E.M. Storms, in his book 'Should a Christian be a Mason?' (p. 43) states, "Nowhere in Masonry is the 'brother' more cleverly deceived than in the presentation of its varied and ancient symbols. Most symbols are dualistic in nature and Masonic symbols are no exception. Behind all Masonic symbolism there is an undisclosed occult interpretation of which most Freemasons are ignorant."

The ironic fact is both evangelical and Masonic authorities are at complete agreement on the deceptive nature of secret society symbolism. The most authoritative Masonic writer ever, was held to be Albert Pike (1809-1891). He rose to Sovereign Grand Commander of the Supreme Council of the thirty-third degree (Mother council of the World) and Supreme Pontiff of Universal Freemasonry. In his book 'Morals and Dogma' (accepted universally as 'the bible' of Freemasonry) Pike admits: "Masonry like all religions, all the Mysteries, Hermeticism and Alchemy, conceals its secrets from all except the Adepts and Sages, or the Elect and uses *false explanations and misinterpretations of its symbols to mislead those who deserve to be misled*; to conceal the Truth which it calls Light, from them, and to draw them away from it."

He further states, "The Blue Degrees are but the outer court or portico of the Temple. *Part of the symbols are displayed there to the Initiate, but he is intentionally misled by false interpretations. It is not intended that he shall understand them, but it is intended that he shall imagine he understands them*" ('Final Notice' by Barry Smith pp. 328-329).

It is these dualistic symbols, which the Royal Arch Purple has foolishly received from Freemasonry, that are subtly elevated today as honourable symbols of Protestantism. Such folly can never be, as they disguise a hidden occult significance, and are in reality the devil's dirty imprints.

the ark of God

'The Ark of the Covenant', also known in Scripture as 'the Ark of the Lord', 'the Ark of God' and 'the Ark of the testimony' served as a hallowed symbol of the Divine presence in the midst of the children of Israel. It was also a tangible representation of the truth and power of Almighty God. It contained the sacred 'mercy seat' as its covering, a typical Old Testament picture of Christ and His atoning work on Calvary. Amazingly the Royal Arch Purple blasphemously teach (during its initiation) that this sacred symbol 'the-Ark-of-God' really represents G-O-A-T spelt backwards. This sacrilegious perverting of holy things within the Order further shows the esoteric (or occult) nature of the Institution.

The Royal Arch Purple, like the foolish Philistines in 1 Samuel 5:2, have attempted to bring this sacred symbol of God's presence (the Ark of God) into the (heathen) house of Dagon. However, we learn in Scripture that after this holy representation was placed within an alien structure, "Dagon was fallen upon his face to the earth before the Ark of the Lord." (V. 3) This highlights the fact that when the *presence and power* of Almighty God is placed in the midst of iniquity, the counterfeit cannot truly stand, because in reality, truth and error can never co-exist!

the all-seeing eye

The Royal Arch Purple employs a mystical eye in its imagery known throughout the occult world as "the all-seeing eye." This symbol which is shared with most false religions, cults and occult bodies today has always been used as a symbol of 'deity'. Occultist Fredrick Goodman explains that, "The eye plays a most important part in occult symbolism and probably owes its origin in western magical designs to the Eye of Horus, which was one of the most frequently used of Egyptian magical symbols" (Magical Symbols p. 101).

The Masonic third degree lecture teaches that the "All-Seeing Eye whom the Sun Moon and Stars obey, and under whose watchful care even comets perform their stupendous revolutions, beholds the innermost recesses of the human heart, and will reward us according to our works" (Beyond The Light' p. 136).

Here, whilst addressing the subject of the all-seeing eye, Freemasonry once again outlines its erroneous teaching of 'salvation through an upright character and good works'. This is in complete violation of Scripture which teaches: "**Knowing that a man is not justified by the works of the law, but by the faith of Jesus Christ, even we have believed in Jesus Christ, that we might be justified by the faith of Christ, and not by the works of the law: for by the works of the law shall no flesh be justified** " (Galatians 2:16).

Significantly the Royal Arch Purple repeats this false teaching (nearly word for word), by saying, "*The All-Seeing Eye whom the Sun Moon and Stars obey, and under whose watchful care perform their stupendous operations, looks to the innermost thoughts of the heart, and will reward us according to our actions.*"

The peculiar secret society teaching that surrounds this esoteric symbol, not surprisingly, disguises an occult meaning. Evangelical author of 'Guardians of the Grail' J.R. Church states, "*The symbol may represent a god, but it is not the God of the Bible. It is a human eye indicating that man is god. It represents so-called 'mind power', the ability to manipulate one's world with thought*" (p. 165).

Occultist Fredrick Goodman writes that, "the eye relates to the 'God within' to the higher spiritual guardian who can 'see' the purpose of man's life, and in some mysterious way guide him" (Magical Symbols p. 101).

J.R. Church further points out that, "*Many modern groups, though not related through organisation structure, nevertheless, claim to be offshoots of the original so-called Mystery Religion. They practice and believe the same so-called Secret Doctrine. Some organisations may even appear to be enemies, but their underlying philosophy is the same. They appear to be tributaries of the mainstream Babylonian philosophy. They all carry the same symbols, such as* ***the All Seeing Eye****, and believe in the same so-called Secret Doctrine*" (p. 161). He also explains that "*It is the symbol of the Illuminati, as well as the symbol of the Rosicrucians*" (p. 165).

five pointed star

The five-pointed star, known as the pentagram, is probably the most blatant occult symbol in use today. Witches Janet and Stewart Farrar explain that the five-pointed star is "one of the main symbols of witchcraft and occultism in general" ('Hidden Secrets of the Eastern Star' p. 82). The star itself is known by different names throughout the occult world, such as a witch's foot, a goblin's cross, a wizard's star and the dog star. Wiccan witches use its five points to mystically represent the elements of nature - earth, fire, water, air and spirit.

This symbol is one of the most prominent emblems within the Royal Arch Purple, though its significance, like every symbol inherited from Freemasonry, is concealed behind a smokescreen of secret society ambiguity.

The five-pointed star is found on most Arch Purple memorabilia and represents the blasphemous resurrection rite of the five points of fellowship, each point mystically symbolising a part of the resurrection act. First - **F**oot to foot. Second - **K**nee to knee. Third - **H**and in hand. Fourth - **B**reast to breast. Fifth and last - **H**and behind back.

The symbol is normally seen within the Arch Purple with the single point pointing upwards denoting its association, like Masonry and Mormonism, with white witchcraft. Ironically, all these aforementioned bodies employ the heathenish five points of fellowship within their respective initiations.

In the 'Dictionary of Mysticism' by Frank Gaynor we learn that the five-pointed star "is considered by occultists to be the most potent means of conjuring spirits. When a single point of the star points upward, it is regarded as the sign of the good and a means to conjure benevolent spirits; when the single point points down and a pair of points are on top, it is a sign of the evil (Satan) and is used to conjure powers of evil" ('Hidden Secrets of the Eastern Star' p. 84).

Lewis Spence states in 'An Encyclopaedia of Occultism': "*This symbol has been used by all secret and occult societies, by the Rosicrucians, the Illuminati, down to the Freemasons today*" ('Should a Christian be a Mason?' p. 53).

The book of Acts tells us how the disobedient children of Israel brought such imagery into the camp and how God dealt with it: "**Then God turned, and gave them up to worship the host of heaven; as it is written in the book of the prophets, O ye house of Israel, have ye offered to me slain beasts and sacrifices by the space of forty years in the wilderness? Yea, *ye took up the tabernacle of Moloch, and the star of your god Remphan*, figures which ye made to worship them: and I will carry you away beyond Babylon**" (Acts 7:42-43).

sun, moon and stars

The sun, moon and stars, known in Scripture as the host of heaven, are found to be to the fore of Royal Arch Purple imagery. These heathenish emblems, which have always been associated with Baal worship, are also found prominently displayed today within most New Age shops. It is not surprising to find such imagery spread widely throughout the occult world. Paganism has always showed its trinities in art by the sun (with a face) representing the *male* sun god, the moon (with a face) representing the moon goddess (or queen of heaven) and the all-seeing eye representing their offspring.

The children of Israel were often seen turning towards these objects of idolatry at times of great apostasy in Scripture. Such a time is revealed in II Kings 17:16, where "**they left all the commandments of the LORD their God, and made them molten images, even two calves, and made a grove, and worshipped all the host of heaven, and served Baal**."

other symbols employed

The Royal Arch Purple Order use many other esoteric symbols such as the 'blindfold' (c/f. Ch. 3) the 'sword pointing to the heart' (c/f. Ch. 4), a 'mystical ladder' (c/f. Ch. 6), the 'two and a half (c/f. Ch. 6), 'a coffin' (c/f. Ch. 6) and many more. All these symbols carry a hidden occult significance, which can only be comprehended by acquiring esoteric knowledge provided during ritual initiation. This teaching and imagery is common to all secret societies and is shared also with Mormonism and the New Age movement.

summary

Some apologists for the Royal Arch Purple have sheepishly argued, on the general subject of symbolism, that "it is what you take out of it!" But is it? Such an argument, if correct, would lend support to so-called 'evangelical Roman Catholics' partaking of the wafer in the idolatrous mass. After all "it's what you take out of it?" It would also give credence to a deluded Christian wearing a superstitious crucifix round his neck to denote his deep love for Christ. Again "it is what you take out of it?"

Such a liberal position is expounded in the book 'The Orange Order: An Evangelical Perspective', written by Grand Chaplain of the Grand Orange Lodge of Scotland, Arch Purple man and Rev. Ian Meredith and Irish Arch Purple man Rev. Brian Kennaway. With reference to the five-pointed star, they suggest, "*It means what you want it to mean and nothing more*." Referring to the all-seeing eye they repeat their shallow stance, saying, "*The symbol is neutral, it all depends what it means to you*." Holding such an indeterminate logic would force a man to assume an attitude that there are no absolute rights and no absolute wrongs, i.e. secular humanism. This philosophy is at clear variance with the instruction of Scripture, which teaches that there *are* absolute rights and there *are* absolute wrongs.

Other apologists for the Royal Arch Purple even try to liken the Arch Purple symbolism to the occasional symbolism found within some evangelical churches like the dove and the burning bush. Nevertheless, comparing such rare (and open) symbolism to the numerous mystical hidden occult symbols employed within secret societies is contorted in the extreme.

Setting aside such empty reasoning, we see that the Royal Arch Purple has unquestionably received its symbols from a blatant occult source - Freemasonry. Those at the top of the Order today, like those who formed the Order, are fully aware of the true origins and significance of these mystical symbols. Occult symbolism is, in reality, the devil's fingerprints and they can normally be found anywhere he enjoys control.

The Psalmist exposed the same compromise in his day, saying, "**Lift up thy feet unto the perpetual desolations; even all that the enemy hath done wickedly in the sanctuary. Thine enemies roar in the midst of thy congregations*; they set up their ensigns for signs*" (Psalms 74:3-4).

Any Christian owning any secret society memorabilia (whether regalia, books, certificates or artefacts) should destroy them. Deuteronomy 7:25&26 instructs: "**The graven images of their gods shall ye burn with fire: thou shalt not desire the silver or gold that is on them, nor take it unto thee, lest thou be snared therein: for it is an abomination to the LORD thy God. Neither shalt thou bring an abomination into thine house, lest thou be a cursed thing like it: but thou shalt utterly detest it, and thou shalt utterly abhor it; for it is a cursed thing**."

David followed this instruction in 2 Samuel 5:21 after he had defeated the Philistines in the valley of Rephaim. The Bible records: "**And there they** [the Philistines] **left their images, and David and his men burned them** ."

Paul the Apostle was faced with a similar circumstance, in his day, as he preached the Word of God to the Jews and Greeks in Ephesus. This time the Spirit of the Lord convicted the new converts to destroy their accumulated heathen imagery. The Bible says, "**and fear fell on them all, and the name of the Lord Jesus was magnified. And many that believed came, and confessed, and shewed their deeds. Many of them also which used curious arts brought their books together, and burned them before all men: and they counted the price of them, and found it fifty thousand pieces of silver. So mightily grew the word of God and prevailed**" (Acts 19:17-20).

It is high time that Protestantism was purged of every semblance of Baal worship!

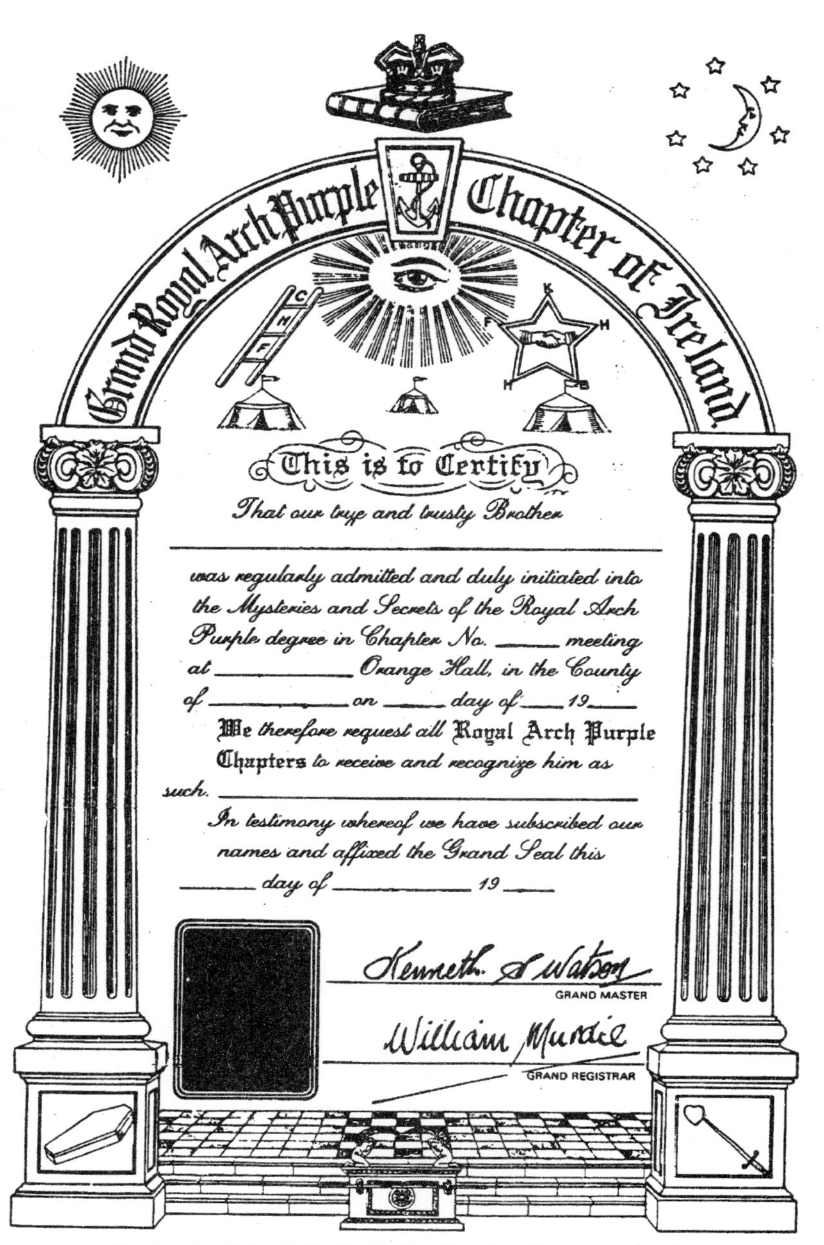

Grand Royal Arch Purple Chapter of Ireland

This is to Certify

That our true and trusty Brother

____

was regularly admitted and duly initiated into the Mysteries and Secrets of the Royal Arch Purple degree in Chapter No. _____ meeting at __________ Orange Hall, in the County of __________ on _____ day of _____ 19____

We therefore request all Royal Arch Purple Chapters to receive and recognize him as such. ______________________________

In testimony whereof we have subscribed our names and affixed the Grand Seal this _____ day of __________ 19____

GRAND MASTER

GRAND REGISTRAR

The Royal Arch Purple Certificate. It outlines how the member has been "initiated into the Mysteries and Secrets of the Royal Arch Purple degree."

conclusion

Man from time immemorial has always tried to serve God on his own terms and in his own way. From the devil-inspired, bloodless sacrifice of Cain to the man-made good works structure of Babel, and even to this day, man has imagined that he can devise a better way than God can.

Satan's most successful deceptions are designed to look and feel the part. Like the imitation shields that disobedient King Rehoboam placed in the house of the Lord, after the enemy had taken the original gold ones, they seem *outwardly* to be the genuine article.

2 Chronicles 12 states, "So Shishak king of Egypt came up against Jerusalem, and took away the treasures of the house of the Lord, and the treasures of the king's house; he took all: he carried away also the shields of gold which Solomon had made. *Instead of which king Rehoboam made shields of brass*, and committed them to the hands of the chief of the guard, that kept the entrance of the king's house" (V. 9-10).

Looking from a distance, brass looks the same as gold, but placed under careful examination it is exposed as nothing better than fool's gold. God makes gold but man manufactures brass. Gold is the genuine, brass is the counterfeit.

In light of the amazing revelations in this book we see a powerful case in point. For many years the Royal Arch Purple Order has succeeded in depicting itself as 'a great bastion of the Protestant Faith which is firmly committed to true scriptural principles'. Nevertheless when put under close examination, and scrutinised in the light of God's Word, this body is exposed for what it is, a subtle man-made counterfeit. It is fool's gold!

With the amount of evangelicals involved in this Order running into thousands, there is little doubt that this pagan edifice has been a hindrance to the blessing of God in our nation. Found behind its closed doors the Arch Purple propagates a gospel that is incompatible with, and contrary to, the Word of God, and employs practices that are clearly alien to evangelical Protestantism. Such compromise is nothing new but has been the hallmark of every spiritual 'falling away' down through the ages. Of course there is "no new thing under the sun" (Ecclesiastes 1:9). In Isaiah 3:8 we learn, "**For Jerusalem is ruined, and Judah is fallen: because *their tongue*** [or language] ***and their doings*** [or endeavours] **are against the LORD, to provoke the eyes of his glory**."

The Bible predicts that such a day would arrive prior to the second coming of the Lord. II Thessalonians 2:3 says: "**Let no man deceive you by any means: for that day** [the second advent] **shall not come, except there come a falling away first**." The term "falling away" used here means a defection from truth and is derived from the Greek word '*apostasia'*, where we significantly obtain our English word APOSTASY.

counterfeit by its very existence

Man-made brotherhoods by their very existence are an anathema to a thrice-holy God. Whilst veiled with religious trappings and outward respectability, they are subtly designed on the devil's drawing board to be an alternative to, and a counterfeit of, the true brotherhood of believers, the Church.

This brotherhood of believers is not only ordered of God, but is created by Him for His glory and the extension of His blessed Kingdom. This body, the Church, is the sole institution ordained of God for the proclamation and defence of the Word of God, and has Christ as its supreme ruling Head. The Bible says, that God "**hath put all things under his feet, and gave him to be the head over all things to the church, Which is his body, the fulness of him that filleth all in all**" (Ephesians 1:22-23).

The human body, so harmoniously fitted together, is presented in Scripture as a beautiful picture of the mystical union between Christ and the Church. By virtue of that union, the child of God enjoys spiritual unity and communion with that body of believers. The Bible says, "**For as the body is one, and hath many members, and all the members of that one body, being many, are one body: so also is Christ**" (1 Corinthians 12:12).

The instrument God uses to bind the believer to Christ is the Holy Spirit. The true believer is indwelt by the Holy Spirit and is therefore joined to Christ through the work of the Spirit. The Bible says, "He that is joined unto the Lord is one spirit" (I Corinthians 6:17). Every believer united to Christ is thus united to His brethren by the Spirit, all being members of the body of Christ. Ephesians 4:16 says, "**The whole body fitly joined together and compacted by that which every joint supplieth**."

Every member has a unique part to play in the development of the body. None are there by chance, all have been the focus of God's special grace and mercy, being chosen in Christ and purchased by His precious blood. The Bible says: "**Ye are bought with a price; be not ye the servants of men**" (1 Corinthians 7:23).

Secret societies by their very existence are an alternative to the body of believers the Church, and thus deprive Christ of His rightful place in men's lives. Found within these institutions are all the component parts of the Church, albeit in imitation form. They even mimic God's people by portraying themselves as a brotherhood, referring to their fellow members as 'brethren' and the individual member as 'brother'. Nevertheless Jesus said, "**For whosoever shall do the will of my Father which is in heaven, the same is my brother, and sister, and mother**" (Matthew 12:50).

Christians have no right to undermine their privileged position within the body of believers by joining such man-made counterfeits. Such compromise, damages their walk with God, weakens their commitment to the body of believers and flies in the face of Scripture.

The Bible commands: "**Honour all men, Love the brotherhood, Fear God, Honour the King**" (I Peter 2:17). John Gill, in expounding this passage, explains, "Love the brotherhood; or 'your brethren'.... the whole company of the brethren in Christ, who are born of God, are members of Christ, and of the same body, and have the same spirit, belong to the same family, and are of the household of faith."

The Bible instructs the believer to "do good unto all men, **especially unto them who are of the household of faith**" (Galatians 6:10). The child of God's position within the brotherhood of believers negates any need for man-made imitations.

counterfeit by its nature

The secret false practices of the Royal Arch Purple expose the counterfeit nature of the Order. Such secrecy runs against the Lord's plan for His Church, which was designed to be a just, open and outward-reaching body. Jesus said in Mark 16:15: "**Go ye into all the world, and preach the gospel to every creature**."

In a desperate attempt to justify the spurious secrecy practised within the Order, prominent Royal Arch Purple men Rev. Ian Meredith and Rev. Brian Kennaway state in their book 'The Orange Order: An Evangelical Perspective' (p. 15): "*Towards the end of his life on earth our Lord engaged in a system of secrecy, passwords and signs*." Such teaching blatantly violates God's infallible Word and is devoid of *any* scriptural warrant.

Our Lord's own earthly ministry was an impeccable example for all that would truly follow Him. Jesus said, "**I spake openly to the world; I ever taught in the synagogue, and in the temple, whither the Jews always resort; and in secret have I said nothing**" (John 18:20). Both our Lord's life and His teaching exposed secret (clandestine) behaviour. Jesus said, "**For there is nothing hid, which shall not be manifested; neither was any thing kept secret, but that it should come abroad**" (Mark 4:22).

The Protestant Reformers acted upon our Lord's instruction. They were not a secret select band of elitists who, having obtained the light of the Gospel, selfishly hid it behind closed doors. They were a band of men and women, saved by the grace of God, who let their light so shine before men. Jesus said, "**No man, when he hath lighted a candle, putteth it in a secret place, neither under a bushel, but on a candlestick, that they which come in may see the light**" (Luke 11:33).

The Lord clearly commands His people, the Church, to be open and outward-reaching in their ministry. This Divine teaching is in complete contrast to the Royal Arch Purple Order who significantly commands its people to *conceal and never reveal its teaching and practices to anyone, save fellow Royal Arch Purple men.*

Most secret societies seem uncomfortable with the label 'secret society'; they seem to fall over themselves to disprove they warrant such a description. The *Masonic* Grand Lodge of Ireland in a recent publication called 'The Christian and the Craft', written by prominent Freemason Rev. Warren Porter, states: "It is, of course, the most glaring of misnomers to call Freemasonry a Secret Society. Like almost every other Society, it has its own private concerns, secrets if one wishes to use the word. But that is something altogether different from being a 'Secret Society'. Masonic meeting places are well known. The time of assembly can be easily verified. The leading officers are known, and often highly public figures." He then compares the secrecy practised by Freemasonry, to the just confidentiality practised by Church sessions "when the nature of business requires that matters be dealt with in that way."

No one analysing the sinful secrecy practised by the Royal Arch Purple and other similar societies could compare it to the *legitimate confidentiality*, which is *sometimes* used within the Church, a business, or government to protect *sensitive lawful decisions*. Such an erroneous argument highlights the hypocrisy of these secret bodies.

Why, if the Royal Arch Purple and other secret fraternities are so biblical, do they need to hide their teaching and practices behind a thick wall of secrecy, mystery and deception? The truth is, such secrecy is essential to the very existence of these secret societies as it protects their spurious practices and false doctrines. It conceals such from outside examination and therefore minimises any condemnation or embarrassment. Internally, secrecy maintains a sense of exclusiveness among its members, which makes them feel part of an elite group of individuals.

John Robison in a book 'Proofs of a Conspiracy' explains the importance of secrecy to secret societies. In it he quotes a letter written by the founder of the Illuminati, and former Jesuit Priest, Adam Weishaupt: "Secrecy gives greater zest to the whole… the slightest observation shows that nothing will so much contribute to increase the zeal of the members as secret union."

William T. Still in his evangelical book 'New World Order: - The Ancient Plan of Secret Societies' (p. 45) explains that there are two main reasons why secret orders, down through the years, have employed secrecy. "First was to prevent condemnation and persecution in the event the rites they practised were made public. A second purpose for secret societies was to create a mechanism for the perpetuation, from generation to generation, of policies, principles, or systems of learning, confined to a limited group of selected and initiated persons."

Secrecy is the very lifeblood of the occult world; in fact the actual word occult means 'hidden' or 'secret'. The word is derived from the Latin word 'occultus' meaning secret, and 'occulere' meaning to conceal or to hide. It is always the aim of occultism to conceal and to hide their practices from 'the profane' and from public scrutiny. Dedicated occultists state that the occult is primarily concerned with providing mystical enlightenment and illumination. This is only achieved by secret knowledge gained through ritual initiation.

Secrecy has always been at the core of Satan's ancient mysteries. The Rev. Alexander Hislop in his book 'The Two Babylons' states: "*If idolatry was to continue - if, above all, it was to take a step in advance, it was indispensable that it should operate in secret... In these circumstances, then, began, there can hardly be a doubt, that system of 'Mystery' which, having Babylon for its centre, has spread over the world. In these Mysteries, under the seal of secrecy and the sanction of an oath, and by means of all the fertile resources of magic, men were gradually led back to all the idolatry that had been publicly suppressed.*"

The importance of protecting secrecy within the occult world is explained by occultist Andre Nataf in his book 'The Occult' (p. 81). He states: "*Unveiling the secret and putting it in the public domain drains 'force and vigour' from the hermetic ceremony* in progress and from the initiating group the person belongs to."

Nataf continues: "*Esoteric knowledge must be kept secret. The adept passing on his knowledge to a disciple or the secret society carrying out an initiation ceremony both demand, under pain of retribution, - and they often seal the promise with the swearing of a solemn oath - that nothing of what is learnt will be revealed to the profane.*"

We can clearly see that, where the enemy is at work, secrecy and bondage is to the fore, whereas, as the Scriptures declare, "**Where the Spirit of the Lord is, there is liberty**" (2 Corinthians 3:17). Such unscriptural secrecy only effectively exists when coupled with the vulgar imposition of fear and bondage.

From the very commencement of the initiation, the Royal Arch Purple candidate enters into a mystical world of secrecy and spiritual bondage. The Order extricates an unjust oath of binding loyalty from the ignorant candidate before he is even initiated, to never reveal and ever conceal the teachings of the Order. During the ceremony they even place the candidate on a representation of a coffin to show that he would rather suffer death and all its penalties before he would divulge anything he had received, or was about to receive.

Later in the ceremony the candidate learns the consequence of divulging the practices and teaching of the Royal Arch Purple to others - that of having his throat cut across from ear to ear, his tongue torn out by its roots and his left breast torn open, his heart and vitals taken therefrom, etc. etc.

The awful profanity of such penalties reveals the horrible depths to which the Royal Arch Purple Order will sink to secure its superstitious secrets and mysteries. Such wickedness is unquestionably exercised to govern the spirit and moral conscience of all those that enter its doors.

The afore-mentioned curses reveal the sinister nature of the Royal Arch Purple and destroy any credence they have for projecting themselves as 'Defenders of the Protestant Faith'. Ironically, the threats of mutilation contained in the penalties are addressed to any member within the Order who would simply share the teaching and practices of the body with others.

Those men who are responsible for administering these wicked curses, whether wantonly or not, are clearly active on the devil's business. Jesus said, "**The thief** [Satan] **cometh not, but for to steal, and to kill, and to destroy: I am come that they might have life, and that they might have it more abundantly**" (John 10:10).

No blood-bought child of God has the right to bind himself to such sin. The Bible says: "**Stand fast therefore in the liberty wherewith Christ hath made us free, and be not entangled again with the yoke of bondage** " (Galatians 5:1).

Christians who subject themselves to the evil influence of these secret bodies serve only to undermine the precious redeeming work that Christ has accomplished for them at that place called Calvary. Jesus said: "**If the Son therefore shall make you free, ye shall be free indeed**" (John 8:36).

Any member of the Arch Purple bound by a fear of the Order must heed the comforting words of Christ, in Scripture: "**Fear them not therefore: for there is nothing covered, that shall not be revealed; and hid, that shall not be known. What I tell you in darkness, that speak ye in light: and what ye hear in the ear, that preach ye upon the housetops** " (Matthew 10:26-27).

counterfeit by its teaching

The Royal Arch Purple Order continues to portray itself as a 'bulwark of the Protestant Faith', which is firmly committed to scriptural practices and principles. The Royal Arch Purple Chapter in its book 'History of the Royal Arch Purple Order' even describes itself, to the readership, as "an Order that is soundly based on Holy Scriptures" (p. 192).

Despite deceptive statements to the contrary, it is abundantly clear that the Royal Arch Purple propagates a gospel that is alien to the truth of God's Word. Throughout the whole Royal Arch Purple degree the Order is constantly found corrupting the truth of the Word by misusing, misapplying and misquoting Holy Scripture. They continually persist in adding to the infallible truths of the Bible, thus creating another counterfeit gospel. The Bible says: **"To the law and to the testimony: if they speak not according to this word, it is because there is no light in them"** (Isaiah 8:20).

William T. Still says: "Masonry, like other secret societies, is set up with an 'outer' doctrine for consumption by the general public, and an 'inner' secretive doctrine known only to an elect few" (New World Order: The Ancient Plan of Secret Societies. p. 28).

Right from its inception, the Royal Arch Purple Order has deceptively tried to fuse the just principles of evangelical Protestantism with the false teaching of pagan Masonry.

This folly is defended by Rev. Ian Meredith and Rev. Brian Kennaway. In their book 'The Orange Order: An Evangelical Perspective' they deceptively tell the reader: "*The Royal Arch Purple degree of Orangeism is based on Scripture, with no mythology or non Biblical material.*" They then boldly state: "*Orangeism could be described as a Christianised or 'Reformed Freemasonry' with the unscriptural and erroneous bits cut out and the movement brought into line with evangelical doctrine*" (pp. 12, 25).

Frankly, Freemasonry can no more be Christianised or Reformed than paganism. In reality, rather than 'Protestantising' Freemasonry the Royal Arch Purple are 'paganising' the Reformed Faith. This subtlety of mingling truth with error is nothing new and is designed by the devil to dilute the infallible authority of God's Word.

God has always judged His people when they tried to merge 'the true faith' with that of the enemy. The children of Israel received such a rebuke in Psalm 106:34-36. It says, "**They did not destroy the nations, concerning whom the LORD commanded them: But were mingled among the heathen, and learned their works. And they served their idols: which were a snare unto them**."

Evangelical Protestantism is, by its very nature, totally incompatible with Freemasonry. Whilst Masonry has evolved from the false teaching of Satan's ancient mysteries, Protestantism has grown from the truth of God's Word: The Protestant Reformation being built upon three great principles, 'Sola Scriptura' - By Scripture alone, 'Sola Gratia' - By Grace alone, 'Sola Fide' - By Faith alone.

The Bible clearly says, "**What concord hath Christ with Belial? or what part hath he that believeth with an infidel? And what agreement hath the temple of God with idols?**" (2 Corinthians 6:15-16).

The Reformers believed in the purity, simplicity and all-sufficiency of the Word of God. They held the Bible to be the inerrant, infallible, fully inspired Word of Truth and believed it to be the final authority on all matters of faith and conduct. They submitted themselves to the teaching of Scripture, abandoning the vain teachings and inventions of man.

Lorraine Boettner in his book 'Roman Catholicism' (p. 90) outlines, "The primary and almost immediate result of the Reformation was to bring the doctrines of Scripture clearly before men's minds as the Reformers based their teaching squarely on the scriptures to the exclusion of all accumulated tradition."

Proverbs 30:5-6 says, "**Every word of God is pure: he is a shield unto them that put their trust in him. Add thou not unto his words, lest he reprove thee, and thou be found a liar**."

Ironically many thousands of our forefathers laid down their lives to uphold the supreme authority and open spread of God's precious Word, whereas today we are faced with this subtle invention, in the guise of Protestantism, which is nonchalantly corrupting and concealing the truth of God's precious Book.

The great Scottish Reformer John Knox declared the evangelical Protestant position on Holy Writ, in his famous encounter with the devout Roman Catholic Queen Mary, at Holyrood Palace, Edinburgh. When asked by the Queen: "You interpret the Scriptures in one way and they [the Church of Rome] in another: whom shall I believe, and who shall be judge?"

Knox replied, "You shall believe God, who plainly speaketh in his word, and farther than the word teacheth you, you shall believe neither the one nor the other" (Life of John Knox p. 175).

Any institution purporting to be an adherent of the Protestant Faith must first submit itself to the supreme authority of God's infallible Word. On this overriding test, the Royal Arch Purple stands naked, exposed and condemned. Consistently throughout their ceremony the Order is found tampering with, and adding to biblical truth. These practices unquestionably violate the instruction of Scripture which states, "**Ye shall not add unto the word which I command you, neither shall ye diminish ought from it**" (Deuteronomy 4:2).

Clearly no one has the authority to tamper with the infallible truth of God's Word the result of such behavior is always a watered down counterfeit gospel. The Bible says "**If any man preach any other gospel unto you than that ye have received, let him be accursed**" (Galatians 1:9).

Charles H. Spurgeon so succinctly outlined the evangelical position on Scripture, when he said: "*The Bible, the whole Bible and nothing but the Bible.*"

The "gospel" which the Royal Arch Purple employs, clearly violates the truth and simplicity of God's Word and is therefore, by nature, anti-Protestant. The Order has no right to appropriate the name Protestant to justify its pagan practices. Such a craftily devised construction is ultimately designed to undermine the Protestant Faith rather than strengthen it.

The Westminster Confession of Faith (Ch 1 sec 10) is clear. "The supreme judge by which all controversies of religion are to be determined, and all decrees of councils, opinions of ancient writers, doctrines of men, and private spirits, are to be examined; and in whose sentence we are to rest; can be no other but the Holy Spirit speaking in the Scripture."

There is little doubt from the evidence before us that the Royal Arch Purple teaching is a deceptive counterfeit. Whilst the Order outwardly portrays Protestantism, she inwardly practises paganism. Iraneaus, Bishop of Lyon, France (2nd Century AD) once declared, "Error is never set forth in its naked deformity lest it being thus exposed it should be detected; but is craftily decked out in attractive dress so as by its outward form to make it appear to the inexperienced, more truth than truth itself" ('The World's Last Dictator' p. 151).

The Lord Jesus Christ said, "**This people draweth nigh unto me with their mouth, and honoureth me with their lips; but their heart is far from me. But in vain they do worship me, teaching for doctrines the commandments of men**" (Matthew 15:8-9).

Former Wiccan Witch High Priest and thirty-second degree Freemason, William J Schnoebelen poignantly states: "If the devil can preach my sermons without changing them much, what does that say about my sermons?"

Men, under the guidance of Satan, have always questioned the infallible authority of Scripture. The Lord exposed such agents of hell, when He said, "**Ye are of your father the devil, and the lusts of your father ye will do. He was a murderer from the beginning, and abode not in the truth, because there is no truth in him. When he speaketh a lie, he speaketh of his own: for he is a liar, and the father of it**" (John 8:44).

counterfeit by its practices

The Reformation dealt a shattering blow to ritualism within the Church because the Reformers believed in the supreme authority and simplicity of the Word of God. To such an end they purged out all the ritualistic false practices of Rome and replaced them with a simple living faith in the risen Lord.

Lorraine Boettner in his book 'Roman Catholicism' explains: "Protestantism has the truth, due largely to its emphasis on the reading and study of the Bible. That truth is set forth as a life to be lived, not as a formula or a ritual.

Its emphasis is upon a change of heart and a life of fruitful service" (p. 297).

Evangelical Protestantism is, by its very character, opposed to ritualism within 'the faith'. The great J.C. Ryle in his book 'What do we owe to the Reformation?' reflected that position when he said: "***RITUALISM IS THE HIGHWAY TO ROME***."

Lorraine Boettner further writes: "Elaborate ritual and ceremony, which theoretically are designed to aid the worshipper, usually have the opposite effect in that they tend to take the mind away from things which are spiritual and eternal and to centre it on that which is material and temporal. Artistic ritual...often become ends in themselves, and can easily become instruments which prevent the people from joining in the worship of God" (p. 273).

This elaborate, highly ritualistic, Arch Purple initiation clearly belongs far outside the bounds of evangelical Protestantism. Such an outrageous theatrical display becomes a barrier to truth for the initiate rather than an appropriate channel to reach him. This type of nonsense is contrary to the traditional mode of service that Protestants have always enjoyed. In no place in Scripture do we see any semblance of instruction for believers to behave in such an unseemly manner. As evangelicals we must therefore oppose such evil encroachments. God's Word says: "**What thing soever I command you, observe to do it: thou shalt not add thereto, nor diminish from it**" (Deuteronomy 12:32).

As we scrutinise the degrading Royal Arch Purple ceremony we ultimately find an ancient, alien, pagan edifice manufactured by men of 'another spirit', who designed it to lure the ignorant away from the truth and simplicity of 'the faith' rather than closer to it. The Bible says, "**For there are certain men crept in unawares, who were before of old ordained to this condemnation, ungodly men, turning the grace of our God into lasciviousness, and denying the only Lord God, and our Lord Jesus Christ.... Woe unto them! for they have gone in the way of Cain, and ran greedily after the error of Balaam for reward**" (Jude v4&11).

Grand Secretary of the Grand Orange Lodge of Ireland William J. Gwynn said on 4th January 1878 that the Orange Institution was "*disgraced by members professing to obey its laws, yet jesuitically and secretly adding these silly devices.*" He affirmed, "*They love darkness rather than light, for did they come to the light they would incur the hazard of criminal prosecution by the law of the land. Such ignoring of the Orange laws is the parallel of Ritualism in our Church, whereby Christ's Gospel is ignored, and blind man's invention substituted.*"

This degrading ceremony, which was, clearly, so offensive to Orangeism in the 1800s is still contaminating the Protestant people today. It is of such an extreme and depraved nature that it must be viewed as not just an attack upon the Reformed Faith but also upon human decency. There is surely no reasonable citizen throughout our land, (whether saved or unsaved) who cannot see the destructive force of such an initiation. This rite, which not only strips a man of his clothes but also of his self-respect, must be rooted out of the midst of the Protestant camp lest it *remain* an obstacle to the blessing of God in our land. It would certainly take a depraved mind to contend that this degree could in *anyway* advance the glorious cause of Christ.

Occult author Andre Nataf in his book 'The Occult' reveals the real significance of ritual initiation when he states, "To be initiated is to set off on the trail of an occult truth, which not all can perceive. *Initiation is a ritually transmitted process*" (p. 81).

The Royal Arch Purple Order is, in reality, paganism in disguise. Only Satan could devise a ceremony, which could so commonly be shared throughout the world by Protestant Arch Purple men, Masons and Witches alike. The Bible warns, "**Be sober, be vigilant; because your adversary the devil, as a roaring lion, walketh about, seeking whom he may devour: Whom resist stedfast in the faith, knowing that the same afflictions are accomplished in your brethren that are in the world**" (1 Peter 5:8-9).

It is amazing to see the ease and the extent to which the devil has infiltrated Protestantism today with this shameful structure. It is even more disturbing to see the amount of professing Christians who are drawn into such blatant error. Satan, by subtly labelling the Order 'Protestant' has craftily lured many unsuspecting men into this destructive spiritual bondage. Sadly, many professing believers have been so deluded they are found, today, defending such heathenism, as if it were somehow an integral part of evangelical Protestantism.

Founder of the Illuminati organisation and former Jesuit Priest Adam

Weishaupt once boasted, "The most wonderful thing of all is that the distinguished Lutheran and Calvinist theologians who belong to our Order [the Illuminati] really believe that they see in it the true and genuine sense of the Christian religion. Oh, mortal man, is there any thing you cannot be made to believe?" ('The Worlds Last Dictator' p. 15).

Such language is very significant when viewed in relation to the strong statement which the Grand Orange Lodge of Ireland released in 27th January 1813 which addressed the sinister nature of the Royal Arch Purple degree and those clandestine characters who promoted it. Grand Lodge outlined: "*These were the very Practices and Ceremonies of the Illuminati of France and Germany, who brought their country to Slavery and Ruin. Ask them, how such Practices can conduce to the Maintenance of the Protestant cause, to the Advancement of Loyalty, or the Good of People*?"

The Orange Institution, in a pamphlet released in 1875 called 'Orangeism: Its principles, its purposes and its relation to society - Defined and defended', outlined its clear position on ritualism in that day: "*Ritualism should not be left an inch of ground nor a foot to stand on within the domain of Protestantism, a little leaven leavens the whole lump. There is no necessity for keeping on parallel lines with the heresies of Rome...Protestants should studiously avoid the pit-falls of Rome as they would an epidemic. Too close a similarity to her doctrines, rituals and Church discipline have proved contagious ...where Orangeism flourishes, ritualism cannot gain a footing.*"

The degrading practices of the Royal Arch Purple Order are in such stark contrast to the life and teaching of the Lord Jesus Christ that one can easily discern that the enemy has sown tares. Significantly, no one ever treated the individual with more compassion and respect than the Lord did. Any man involved in this obscene behaviour must therefore follow our Lord's example and the instruction of His Word, and separate from such indecency.

The Bible says, "**As ye have therefore received Christ Jesus the Lord, so walk ye in him: Rooted and built up in him, and stablished in the faith, as ye have been taught, abounding therein with thanksgiving. Beware lest any man spoil you through philosophy and vain deceit, after the tradition of men, after the rudiments of the world, and not after Christ**" (Colossians 2:6-8).

counterfeit way of salvation

Hidden beneath the elaborate ritualism and corrupt teaching of the Royal Arch Purple initiation is a carefully concealed counterfeit path of salvation. This peculiar ceremony which is, amazingly, shared with nearly every cult and occult body throughout the world, is an anathema to biblical truth and therefore *true* evangelical Protestantism.

Satan's greatest deceptions are normally well camouflaged behind a smoke screen of apparent respectability. For them to succeed, the devil knows they must first look the part and secondly work. As we penetrate behind the deceitful outward 'Protestant' trappings of this carefully constructed degree, we find a mystical heathenistic rite, which is designed to counterfeit and undermine the Christian new birth experience.

The fundamental object, at the heart of all occult ceremonies, is to provide 'mystical enlightenment and secret knowledge through ritual initiation'. Such is achieved by taking the candidate on a mysterious journey 'from darkness to light'. The deluded candidate has thus succeeded in taking a progressive step towards satanic illumination.

William T. Still in his evangelical book 'New World Order: - The Ancient Plan of Secret Societies' says: "There are many ways to achieve illumination. The method most important to Illuminists is the mystical inspiration invoked by the performance of occult rituals" (p. 37).

The Royal Arch Purple degree, regardless of how men package it, is an abominable, counterfeit path of salvation. Rather than drawing men to Christ through simple faith, they deceptively and selfishly drag disciples after themselves. Instead of presenting a simple living Gospel where sinners see their need of the Saviour, the Royal Arch Purple confer a damning elaborate alternative.

(the evidence!)

The Royal Arch Purple candidate cannot come to the Order of his own accord; he must be asked. Similarly, no sinner can come to the Lord Jesus Christ of his own accord; he must first be drawn of the Father. Jesus said: "**No man can come to me, except the Father which hath sent me draw him: and I will raise him up at the last day**" (John 6:44).

The Royal Arch Purple candidate comes to the Order in a 'profane, humble and unworthy state'. Similarly, the sinner comes to the Lord Jesus Christ in such a helpless state. The Bible states, "**For all have sinned, and come short of the glory of God**" (Romans 3:23).

The Royal Arch Purple candidate comes into union with the Chapter through the instrument of the obligation. Whilst the sinner comes into union with Christ through the instrument of the Holy Spirit. The Bible says, "**Know ye not that your body is the temple of the Holy Ghost which is in you, which ye have of God, and ye are not your own? For ye are bought with a price: therefore glorify God in your body, and in your spirit, which are God's**" (1 Corinthians 6:19-20).

The Royal Arch Purple candidate goes through a counterfeit re-birth experience in the Royal Arch Purple initiation. The repentant sinner however, is truly born-again of the Spirit of God. Jesus said, "**Verily, verily, I say unto thee, Except a man be born of water and of the Spirit, he cannot enter into the kingdom of God. That which is born of the flesh is flesh; and that which is born of the Spirit is spirit**" (John 3:5-6).

The Royal Arch Purple candidate is brought from a so-called life of darkness into a counterfeit life of light through the Royal Arch Purple initiation, whereas the repentant sinner is brought from a life of darkness into a genuine life of marvellous light through the Lord Jesus Christ. Jesus said, "**I am the light of the world, he that followeth me shall not walk in darkness, but shall have the light of life**" (John 8:12).

The Royal Arch Purple candidate submits himself to the Royal Arch Purple Order and its many ungodly members above other earthly commitments, and even cements that deep commitment by declaring that he would rather suffer death and all its penalties than betray the Order. The repentant sinner consecrates his life to the Lord Jesus Christ, regardless of the cost. The totally surrendered believer can even say with Paul: "**I am set for the defence of the gospel.... According to my earnest expectation and my hope, that in nothing I shall be ashamed, but that with all boldness, as always, so now also Christ shall be magnified in my body, whether it be by life, or by death. For to me to live is Christ, and to die is gain**" (Philippians 1:17,20-21).

The Royal Arch Purple candidate assumes new loyalties, new restraints and a new lifestyle, but the sinner who truly comes to Christ experiences newness of life made possible by the indwelling Holy Spirit. The Bible says "**If any man be in Christ, he is a new creature: old things are passed away; behold, all things are become new**" (2 Corinthians 5:17).

The Royal Arch Purple candidate is presented, at the end of his initiation, with a Christless hope of 'eternal bliss' and a 'heavenly abode'. Whereas every believer receives a blessed assurance from Christ in John 14:1-3: "**Let not your heart be troubled: ye believe in God, believe also in me. In my Father's house are many mansions: if it were not so, I would have told you. I go to prepare a place for you. And if I go and prepare a place for you, I will come again, and receive you unto myself; that where I am, there ye may be also.**"

Article VI of the established Church of England's 'Thirty Nine Articles' states: "Holy Scripture containeth all things necessary to salvation: so that whatsoever is not read therein, nor may be proved thereby, is not to be required of any man, that it should be believed as an article of the Faith, or to be thought requisite or necessary to salvation."

Secret societies present salvation as a process of gradual enlightenment rather than "the complete deliverance that God, through the person and work of Christ, and by the operation of the Holy Spirit, gives to His people" (Dictionary of Theological Terms by Dr. Alan Cairns p. 324). Thus the candidate foolishly undertakes a process of mystical initiations in search of 'revelation' and 'light' (which quite often takes years), each step of this journey being known as a degree. It is because of this lengthy process that a secret society candidate is known as an initiate. Such is in stark contrast to a convert, who receives enlightenment in an *act* of God's sovereign free grace.

Masonic authority Albert Mackey explains the origins and significance of the 'degree' in 'A Lexicon of Freemasonry' (p. 72) stating, "In all the Pagan mysteries, there were progressive degrees of initiation...The object of these steps of probation was to test the character of the aspirant, and at the same time to prepare him, by gradual revelations, for the important knowledge he was to receive at the final moment of his adoption." Secret society make no mention whatsoever of the term 'convert' in their ceremonies, yet they continually refer to their members as aspirants, candidates or initiates.

The whole 'initiation experience' and 'degree system' runs contrary to scriptural pattern and is therefore alien to evangelical Protestantism. True biblical justification is not a process but an act. The act of justification is often explained as – "just as if I never sinned." The Bible states, "**Therefore being justified by faith, we have peace with God through our Lord Jesus Christ**" (Romans 5:1). The Westminster Confession of Faith 'Shorter Catechism' (Ch.11. Q.33) addresses the subject, stating, "Justification is an *act* of God's free grace, wherein He pardoneth all our sins, and accepteth us as righteous in His sight, only for the righteousness of Christ imputed to us, and received by faith alone."

The Royal Arch Purple Order continually fails the test of Scripture, and is therefore contrary to the evangelical Protestant Faith. Believers must therefore contend for the supremacy of God's Word and cut out this heretical cancer which is eating away at the very vitals of true Protestantism. Paul the Apostle wrote in 2 Corinthians 11:3-4: "**I fear, lest by any means, as the serpent beguiled Eve through his subtilty, so your minds should be corrupted from the simplicity that is in Christ**." The child of God is then admonished to separate from those who preach "**another Jesus, whom we have not preached, or if ye receive another spirit, which ye have not received, or another gospel, which ye have not accepted**."

counterfeit by its roots

There is little doubt from the evidence before us that the Royal Arch Purple has evolved from that child of the mysteries, Freemasonry. Found within her body are all the same heathenish practices, teaching and symbolism that are employed within the first three degrees of Freemasonry. It is clear that the Royal Arch Purple possesses within her frame all the same vulgar traits and deeply infected lifeblood, so characteristic of the parent.

Former Royal Arch Purple man George Kershaw was one of the twenty most prominent Orangemen gauged for his opinion on the Royal Arch Purple Order between the years 1876 and 1878. He testified to his shock at receiving an internal Masonic document, which showed him the true origins of the Arch Purple degree. He said of it: "The perusal of this work, from which I was permitted to make what extracts I liked, so disgusted me as seeing in it the source of the rites I had just passed through, so analogous are they in many parts, and seeing also therein the result, I firmly resolved to set my face against any further extension of the order beyond the Orange and Purple."

He concludes: "I consider our Orange Fraternity as formed for the special protection of Protestantism as opposed to Paganism wherever found, whether in the form of Babylonish rite and heathen mysteries of the followers of Nimrod, Bacchus, and Semiramis, or the Saturnalia of Pio Nono and the Whore of Rome, both having the same source and paternal derivation; but to take our stand on the Infallible Rock we contend earnestly for the faith once delivered to the saints, and as such *we must root out from our midst this pollution, and have done with the chamber of imagery and witchcraft*. Let us then put on the whole armour, standing shoulder to shoulder, for the truth."

Nearly every line of instruction and every aspect of ceremony, within the Arch Purple Order, has been meticulously appropriated from pagan Masonry which itself has inherited it from the ancient mysteries. This reality violates the truth of Scripture, which says, "**Who can bring a clean thing out of an unclean? NOT ONE**" (Job 14:4).

The Masonic Encyclopaedia (p. 389) explains that a "*ready made doctrine of imitation, is adequate to explain much of the indubitable likeness between all Instituted Mysteries in all places and times, including the modern system of Freemasonry and co-existing Orders. It must not be denied that some of the mysteries reflected one into another and were adapted one from another... there is the great and magisterial fact of a Secret Tradition which itself was reflected from experience. It was the tradition and experience... of new birth, new life, figurative or mystical death, and in fine a resurrection, rendition or return.*"

The great evangelist John Wesley on a visit to Ballymena, County Antrim on Friday 18th June 1773 said of Freemasonry, after reading a strongly worded tract exposing it, "What an amazing banter upon all mankind is Freemasonry! And what a secret is it, which so many concur to keep! From what motive? through fear-or shame to own it?"

One wonders what ***King William of Orange*** would of thought of such heathenism, having ***died on 8th March 1702***, fifteen years <u>*before*</u> (speculative) Freemasonry was formed and one hundred years <u>*before*</u> this iniquitous Royal Arch Purple degree was formed.

Whilst many within the Royal Arch Purple will cry out against the subtle advances of Roman Catholicism, they themselves hypocritically partake in an Order which has ultimately stemmed from the same Babylonian fountainhead. Alas, how subtle the devil is!

Evangelical author of 'Guardians of the Grail' J.R. Church declares, "*Many modern groups, though not related through organisation structure, nevertheless, claim to be offshoots of the original so-called Mystery Religion. They practice and believe the same so-called Secret Doctrine. Some organisations may even appear to be enemies, but their underlying philosophy is the same. They appear to be tributaries of the mainstream Babylonian philosophy*" (p. 161).

Evangelicals Erwin Lutzer and John DeVries expose the devil's subtle tactics in their book 'Satan's Evangelistic Strategy For This New Age'. They state, "Those who promote the New Age Movement believe that there can be no universal theology, the religions of the world have contradictions that cannot be resolved...The conviction is that *although a universal theology is not possible, a universal experience is possible - indeed, the religions of the world must unite on experience alone.*"

Unquestionably there are all types of demonic conspiracies at work in these closing last days. The 'religious world' of today is being subtly lured into all sorts of varying counterfeits. Every fundamental truth that believers hold dear, is coming under orchestrated attack. Agents from hell are seen actively undermining every truth that pertains to God's infallible Word. Nevertheless the Lord has a faithful remnant, reserved unto Himself, who would rather die than give in to error.

Courageous proponents of truth have always, *and will always,* be labelled by the world as 'narrow-minded bigots'. Nevertheless, *there are absolute truths in God's Word that can never be compromised*. The believer must therefore resolutely hold to the unchanging promises of Scripture. As the Bible states, "**be strong in the Lord, and in the power of his might. Put on the whole armour of God, that ye may be able to stand against the *wiles*** [or the trickery] **of the devil**" (Ephesians 6:10-11).

Irrespective of those whom the devil has ensnared by this Arch Purple counterfeit, *true* evangelicals must stand against it as strongly and as vocally as they would the encroachments of 'New Age', Rome or ecumenism. After all, error is error in God's eyes.

Satan has certainly succeeded in deluding many into believing that this deceptive Royal Arch Purple Order is sound. Such is far from the truth, and must be strongly disputed. The Scriptures admonish us to, "**have no fellowship with the unfruitful works of darkness** [obscurity or secrecy], **but rather reprove** [or expose] **them**." (Ephesians 5:11) No man, saved or unsaved, has the authority to put the Lord's name to this sin!

Isaiah 28:16 says, "**Therefore thus saith the Lord GOD, Behold, I lay in Zion for a foundation a stone, a tried stone, a precious corner stone, a sure foundation: he that believeth shall not make haste**." The house built upon the sand will always sink, whilst the house built upon the sure foundation of Christ will always stand. 1 Corinthians 3:11 says, "**For other foundation can no man lay than that is laid, which is Jesus Christ**."

appendix a

what should i do as a Royal Arch Purple man?

1. Repent of your sin before the Lord. God's Word says, "**If we confess our sins, He is faithful and just to forgive us our sins, and to cleanse us from all unrighteousness**" (1 John 1:9).

The word "repent", in Scripture, means 'to turn away from sin'. Whenever the Lord brings light to bear on any sin within a man's life, he is faced with a decision, obey or disobey! Psalms 66:18 solemnly warns, "**If I regard iniquity in my heart, the Lord will not hear me**."

Corrie ten Boon once said, "An unrepented sin is a continued sin."

The Lord solemnly declares in that familiar passage in 2 Chronicles 7:14: "**If my people, which are called by my name, shall humble themselves, and pray, and seek my face, and *turn from their wicked ways*; then will I hear from heaven, and will forgive their sin, and will heal their land.**"

2. <u>Renounce</u> the unbiblical Royal Arch Purple oath of obligation audibly before the Lord, and ask Him to destroy any influence that the Arch Purple curses may have over your life and that of your family. The Bible says that the believer has "renounced the hidden things of dishonesty" (2 Corinthians 4:2). The word renounce means to take strong verbal action to reject, cut off, totally disown, or break the legal right of something. A true child of God should not under any circumstances subject himself to such devilish secret society curses. Such wicked ties are clearly unscriptural and must be *verbally* renounced before God. Leviticus 5:4-6 says, "**if a soul swear, pronouncing with his lips to do evil, or to do good, whatsoever it be that a man shall pronounce with an oath, *and it be hid from him*; when he knoweth of it, then he shall be guilty in one of these. And it shall be, when he shall be guilty in one of these things, that he shall confess that he hath sinned in that thing: And he shall bring his trespass offering unto the LORD for his sin which he hath sinned**."

Ask the Lord for the covering of His precious blood over your life and that of your family, for Divine protection.

Psalms 91:1-7 says, "**He that dwelleth in the secret place of the most High shall abide under the shadow of the Almighty. I will say of the LORD, He is my refuge and my fortress: my God; in him will I trust. Surely he shall deliver thee from the snare of the fowler, and from the noisome pestilence. He shall cover thee with his feathers, and under his wings shalt thou trust: his truth shall be thy shield and buckler. Thou shalt not be afraid for the terror by night; nor for the arrow that flieth by day; Nor for the pestilence that walketh in darkness; nor for the destruction that wasteth at noonday. A thousand shall fall at thy side, and ten thousand at thy right hand; but it shall not come nigh thee**."

3. <u>Resign</u> from any institution performing this degree. The Bible says, "**The foundation of God standeth sure, having this seal, The Lord knoweth them that are his. And, Let every one that nameth the name of Christ depart from iniquity**" (2 Timothy 2:19).

Evangelist D.L. Moody once stated: "I do not see how any Christian, most of all a Christian minister can go into these secret lodges with unbelievers. They say they can have more influence for good; but I say they can have more influence for good by staying out of them, and then reproving their evil deeds. You can never reform anything by unequally yoking yourself with ungodly men. True reformers separate themselves from the world" ('Should a Christian be a Mason?' p. 77).

God's Word strongly teaches *separation*, separation from ungodly fellowship, separation from false teaching, separation from sin. The child of God is admonished: "**Wherefore come out from among them, and be ye separate, saith the Lord, and touch not the unclean thing; and I will receive you, And will be a Father unto you, and ye shall be my sons and daughters, saith the Lord Almighty** " (II Corinthians 6:17-18).

Charles H. Spurgeon once said: "A man is known by the company he shuns as well as by the company he keeps."

Finally, Revelation 18:4 commands us, "**COME OUT OF HER, MY PEOPLE THAT YE BE NOT PARTAKERS OF HER SINS, AND THAT YE RECEIVE NOT OF HER PLAGUES**."

Brother, "**the day of the LORD is near in the valley of decision!** " (Joel 3:14).

appendix b

unsaved reader

If you feel your need of the Lord Jesus Christ and long to know the joy of sins forgiven. You must: -

1. ***Realise*** you are a lost, hell deserving sinner. The Bible says, **"For all have sinned, and come short of the glory of God**" (Romans 3:23).

2. ***Receive***, by faith, the Lord Jesus Christ as your own and personal Saviour. The Bible says, "**For whosoever shall call upon the name of the Lord shall be saved**" (Romans 10:13).

3. ***Repent*** of your sin (meaning to turn away from your sin). Jesus said, "**except ye repent, ye shall all likewise perish**" (Luke 13:3).

what to pray

Father in heaven, I realise I am a sinner. I am in need of forgiveness. I believe the Lord Jesus Christ died for my sin. I am willing to turn away from sin. I now invite the Lord Jesus Christ to come into my life as my own and personal Saviour. I am willing by the grace of God to follow and obey Christ as the Lord of my life. This I ask in Jesus precious name. Amen.

Should you desire to know more about God's way of salvation, please write to: -

Evangelical Truth
PO Box 69
Banbridge
BT32 4RS

appendix c

specimen resignation letter

To the Secretary

It is with a degree of sadness that I submit my letter of resignation to the Royal Arch Purple Chapter. Over recent time I have discovered teaching within the Order that is contrary to the infallible truth of God's Word. I have also reflected upon the Arch Purple initiation ceremony and feel that it is most indecent and deeply degrading, and is incompatible with the true Protestant Faith. In the light of my own conscience and the truth of God's Word I believe I must resign. God says in His Word, "What thing soever I command you, observe to do it: thou shalt not add thereto, nor diminish from it" (Deuteronomy 12:32).

I have audibly renounced my oath of obligation and the solemn penalties of the Order before the Lord, as I believe they are sinful. The Bible says, "If a soul swear, pronouncing with his lips to do evil, or to do good, whatsoever it be that a man shall pronounce with an oath, and *it be hid from him*; when he knoweth of it, then he shall be guilty in one of these. And it shall be, when he shall be guilty in one of these things, that he shall confess that he hath sinned in that thing" (Leviticus 5:4-5). I also feel that my remaining within the Order would *compromise* my fellowship with the Lord Jesus Christ, who shed His precious blood for me on Calvary.

In closing, I wish no ill will against anyone within the Order. I do trust that the Chapter will analyse the subject further as they ponder upon the sentiments of this letter.

In Christian love.

appendix d

the Wiccan Witchcraft initiation revealed, and compared to Freemasonry

In 'The Dark Side of Freemasonry' (pp. 165-167) former Wiccan Witch high priest and thirty second degree Freemason, and now evangelical authority on the cults and occult, William J Schnoebelen explains.

"A: Both are built on a foundation system of three degrees, with a few forms of Wicca offering some higher degrees after the third degree has been achieved.

B: Both are secret societies in that both membership rolls are secret, and secrets are kept from the general populace (to a greater or lesser degree) by both religions. Both generally meet in secret, except for rare open and public events.

C: Both have highly ceremonial initiations to pass from one degree to another, including sworn oaths.

D: Both have ceremonial purgings and purifications of their ritual space before commencing any ritual work.

E: The precise similarities between the two groups are that both groups

1. Cause candidates to strip off all secular clothing;
2. Cause the candidate to be divested of all metal;
3. Hoodwink (blindfold) the candidate and ceremonially tie ropes around him (though the form of the tying varies);
4. Cause the candidate to stand in the Northeast corner of the 'temple' in the first degree;
5. Challenge the candidate by piercing their naked chest with a sharp instrument (witches use a sword, Masons, the point of a compass);
6. Challenge the candidate with secret passwords;
7. Lead the candidate blindfolded in a circumambulation (walking round) of the temple; and
8. Require the candidate to swear solemn oaths of secrecy before being given custody of the secrets of the group...
9. Both have a ceremonial unhoodwinking of the candidate, following the oath, before lighted candles that is intended to bring 'illumination'.
10. Both convey to the new initiate the "working tools" pertinent to that degree, and each of their uses are taught to them.
11. In both, the tools have correspondences both in the ceremonial realm and in similarities to human reproduction.
12. Both, in the higher degrees, take the initiate through a ritual death and rebirth experience in which the initiate acts the part of a hero (heroine) of the craft.
13. Both cause the candidate to endure (while being blindfolded) being picked up, spun around, carried around, being jolted or struck from person to person. This is supposed to produce an 'altered state of consciousness'."

William J Schnoebelen states in 'Beyond The Light' (p. 215), "he [the Mason] is spiritually connected to an organisation whose rites can effortlessly slide into witchcraft and devil worship and fit beautifully! If Freemasonry is so godly, how can it possibly be interchanged by both witches and satanists so freely?"

appendix e

the masonic initiation compared to the Royal Arch Purple degree

In the unpublished draft to the 'History of the Royal Arch Purple Order' book, the Order explains how the Royal Arch Purple degree was developed from the "three pre-1800 degrees." They also outline the general content of the degree and compare it to that of Freemasonry. They state that: "There are at least twelve points in the one that can be found in the other." They list them as (1) "The preparation of a candidate." (2) "The taking of an obligation." (3) "The penalties." (4) "The method of gaining entrance." (5) "The hostile reception." (6) "The entrance pass." (7) "The testing of a candidate." (8) "The act of circumambulation." (9) The "interruption on each circuit." (10) "The five points of fellowship." (11) "The three steps." (12) "The revelation of the true light of understanding."

It is not surprising that this revealing passage was conveniently omitted from the published Royal Arch Purple book. Nevertheless, facts are stubborn things!

appendix f

the mormon link

The initiation ceremony into *Temple* Mormonism was derived directly from Freemasonry. The founder of Mormonism, Joseph Smith, was himself a dedicated Freemason who was able to lure many fellow Masons into his new-found body. He used Freemasonry as the model for Mormonism and introduced much of the Order's esoteric practices, teaching and symbols into his cult.

The Mormon Penalties
(identical to the Royal Arch Purple penalties)

The initiation for both bodies takes on a similar form. Shrouded in great secrecy and mystery they share matching passwords, handshakes and door-knocks. They commence their ceremonies with a similar oath of allegiance (which includes a vow of chastity). They divest their candidates of personal (worldly) garments. They subject their candidates to a trying initiation ceremony. The Mormon even goes through the Masonic 'five points of fellowship'. The Mormon also subjects himself to the same evil blood-thirsty penalties for disloyalty to the cult as that of Freemasonry. They finally point their initiates to the same Christless hell.

The Mormon symbols, which are found in their temples, on their literature, and on the individual Mormons under-garments have been acquired, in total, from pagan Masonry. From the sun, moon and stars, and the all-seeing eye, to the five-pointed star and more, the origins of this imagery is clear.

The parallels between Mormonism and the Royal Arch Purple Order are unquestionable and there is little doubt that both bodies are derived from the same polluted source.

appendix g

the largest opinion poll conducted, within Orangeism, on the subject of the Royal Arch Purple degree (1876 -1878)

Leading members of the Grand Orange Lodge of England initiated the largest gauge of senior Orange opinion, on the subject of the Royal Arch Purple Order, between the years 1876 and 1878. This opinion poll was conducted amongst the most prominent and influential Orangemen in the British Isles and was intended to assess their stance on the highly ritualistic Royal Arch Purple degree. This poll was felt essential, so as to counteract an well-organised body of clandestine Orangemen who were planning to foist the Royal Arch Purple degree upon Orangeism.

The response of those gauged was strong, clear and unanimously hostile to the Arch Purple degree. Their resolute views seemed to reflect the feeling that existed at the time within the broader Orange family to this heathenistic degree.

Deputy Grand Chaplain of the Grand Orange Lodge of England, Rev. G.W.

Straton proposed to Grand Lodge: "That it be declared by this Grand Lodge that such words as 'Properly prepared', &c., in the Purple Order Ritual give no authority or countenance to any officer or brother to enforce or enjoin an oral Ritual, or an obligation of any kind, to be used in the Loyal Orange Institution of England, other than the two prescribed Rituals, Orange and Purple, sanctioned by Grand Lodge, held at Liverpool, 1876, for the use of the Amalgamated Lodges of England."

Fellow Deputy Grand Chaplain of the Grand Orange Lodge of England, Dr Badenock supported the Rev. Straton's position in a strongly worded statement, which had the backing of his own individual lodge, stating "that complaints having been made, apparently well founded, that Ritualistic practises are being introduced into the Order which are not in accordance with the constitutional and Christian principles and objects of the body, and are in the opinion of this Lodge **vulgar and degrading, and fitted to alienate the affections of its influential members from the Order and to arrest its prosperity and usefulness**, it is resolved to make an earnest representation to the Imperial Grand Master. The Grand Master, the Deputy Grand Master, and Grand Secretary to use their best efforts to put a stop to the practises referred to."

Dr Babenock's Lodge backed him fully in his resolute stance and co-ordinated this U.K. wide gauge of Orange opinion on the Royal Arch Purple degree.

Lord Enniskillen in his capacity as Imperial Grand Master of the Grand Orange Council stated: "**I strongly recommend every Orangeman keep clear of all the numerous and ridiculous innovations**" (9th January 1878).

Thomas Macklin, Grand Secretary of the Grand Orange Lodge of Scotland outlined: "**Politically all besides the Orange and simple Purple are absolutely useless, but viewed in relation to religion not only are they useless but profane and degrading, and ought to restrain the men who practise them from laughing at the mummeries and buffooneries of Popery**" (22nd January 1878).

Chalmers J. Paton. Grand Master of the Grand Orange Lodge of Scotland stated, "**I am of the opinion that all degrees worked by Orangemen other than the Orange and Purple are spurious and unnecessary**" (17th January 1878).

William P. Foord, Past Deputy Provincial Grand Master, England stated, "There are here many Orangemen who have joined the Order and left it (more than the present paying members), and when I meet them. I find they are ready to help us with money but will not come to Lodge, saying they 'can remain Protestants but not Shakers'. That reply I knew referred to the Arch Purple, and it was one I could not answer as I was myself so much shocked at the Blasphemy of that Order that I have never attended one R.A.P. meeting since nor never will. **I can only account for this mischief springing up by the idea that " an enemy has done this " (i.e. sown the tares), it would be well to see if we can detect who it is - this enemy, burn him out, start afresh, and see if we can't do better. We have a noble organization completely spoilt, capable of doing nothing but 'giving the enemy cause to blaspheme'** " (28th January 1878).

Lord Enniskillen in his capacity as Grand Master of the Grand Orange Lodge of Ireland explained, "**nothing could be more contrary to the rules of the Institution, or more injurious to its interests, and it must be promptly and firmly dealt with, and the practice suppressed...** In my opinion a strong resolution, not merely condemnatory, but prohibitory of this innovation, and enjoying the use of the authorized Ritual only in all the Lodges should be adopted, and a copy of it specially transmitted to every private Lodge in the Kingdom" (Not dated).

William J. Gwynn. Grand Secretary of the Grand Orange Lodge of Ireland argued, "**The heresy (as I maintain it to be) of an oral ritual is as a deadly canker eating out the very vitals of true Orangeism, and if it is not rooted out must work its ruin. I view it all fantastic tomfooleries of Arch-Purple, Black, Scarlet, Green and the like as but unauthorized inventions of self-sufficient spirits loving to have the pre-eminence, and to draw disciples after them. Any allegation that an oral ritual is recognized and strictly enforced by the Grand Lodge of Ireland is absolutely untrue, although there are many who, violating its real principle, unite themselves with those schismatics who by thus dividing are the very worst enemies of the Orange body. That body is disgraced by members professing to obey its laws, yet jesuitically and secretly adding these silly devices... They love darkness rather than light, for did they come to the light they would incur the hazard of criminal prosecution by the law of the land. Such ignoring of the Orange laws is the parallel of Ritualism in our Church, whereby Christ's Gospel is ignored, and blind man's invention substituted**" (4th January 1878).

Chas A. Reeks, Orange Institution, England stated: "I have had a short conversation with one of our clerical brethren, who remarked that the Ritual used when he was admitted to the Purple Order was, in his opinion, quite sufficient to drive any clergyman out of the Institution . . .The rev. gentleman is one of four clerical brethren who were scandalized by the ceremonialism of the Arch-Purple Order, and they have not sat in our Lodge since, nor in any other. Surely this is a drawback to the usefulness of our Institution" (4th January, 1878).

Henry Prigg Orange Institution, England stated, "**if the heathenish and degrading ceremonies, such as I made acquaintance with at ... are prescribed and attempted to be foisted upon all the Lodges, the days Orangeism as a power for good in England are numbered...Let me remark, however, that I believe if some of my men were to be witness of, or be aware of what is going on at some of the other Lodges, they would throw up their membership in disgust. Rites such as the Arch-Purple attract the wrong men into our ranks; we want sober, religious-minded Protestants, not pot-house politicians and practical jokers . . . Let the Pagan practises be prohibited and put out of the Order, and then men not worth having with their tomfoolery will leave us and go elsewhere, and better men will attract to our ranks**. I feel very strongly on these points, and you do I am sure likewise. Believe me, &c" (15th December 1877).

G.E.W. Houlding, Orange Institution, England outlined, "I feel it a privilege and at the same time a duty to add my humble protest against the so-called 'Arch Purple' and other higher orders that are sought to be thrust upon us by some among our number... Not only are many prevented joining our ranks from a misconception of our principles but what is worse, many having joined afterwards leave us through **being made the unwilling actors in a *useless* and to a refined mind a *revolting* ceremonial such as that connected with the 'Arch Purple' and other orders... I feel convinced that if we wish to gain the accession to our ranks of intelligent and right minded men, we shall do so, *not* by enveloping our cause with mysterious and *profitless orders*"** (28th January 1878).

Rev. George W. Straton, Deputy Grand Chaplain of the Grand Orange Lodge of England stated, "Will you kindly enter my protest... against such absurdity and abomination, so very detrimental to the original and regular Orange and Purple Orders according to the printed, scriptural, and admirable forms of admission? ***I think it requires not only a very***

ingenious but a very wicked mind to deduce such ridiculous and indecent performances...I shall only add that unless it is put a stop to immediately the Institution will be broken up - I for one will withdraw" (19th January 1878).

Alexander E. Miller, Deputy Grand Master of the Grand Orange Lodge of England stated, "I quite agree with your dislike to the 'Arch Purple', and, if I can manage it, will be at the Lodge meeting for the discussion" (10th December 1877).

W.H. Torriano, Grand Secretary of the late Orange Association. Great Britain explained: "I have always considered all the various forms of this Order and all the imitations of the other so-called high Orders, **a system of disgusting buffoonery, unworthy of men, gentlemen, and Christians**, contrary to the Orange laws and by their oaths contrary to the laws of the land; and had I known when I joined in 1854 that any such practises existed I would never have joined. These practises when known must prevent gentlemen from joining" (21st January 1878).

Rev. B.D. Aldwell, Orange Institution, England stated, "**I am sure that educated men must look on the ceremony with feelings of contempt and abhorrence**. We should raise our Order, not degrade it. It will never be what it should unless we insist on a written ritual and one as we now have it in accordance with the Word of God" (11th January 1878).

Rev. James Ormiston, Orange Institution, England explained: "For many years I have personally sought to discourage the offensive and irreverent formularies, which in the higher Orders have hitherto prevailed in the Institution.

P.S. - I should add that the Institution has to my certain knowledge lost several clerical Members through the disgust caused by the old ritual" (14th December 1877).

T.B.Hill, Past Provincial Grand Master, England affirmed: "I believe it has caused much harm... I have known much injury done to the cause by members of the high orders. The men (I cannot call them Brothers) who volunteered to divulge the secrets of the Society to O'Connell, in order to assist him in his attacks upon the order were prominent members of the Black Order. The oaths taken are no security, as they are frequently broken and are certainly illegal. **I believe few respectable persons would remain**

amongst us after passing through the ritual required in some degrees " (23rd January 1878).

A.L. Allen, Orange Institution of England, argued, "**I consider the old Arch-Purple Ritual as repulsive to the last degree... It is not enough that it is not enjoined, it should be forbidden. I object to it as being silly and undignified, but most of all as being distinctly profane and irreligious**. Having seen the disastrous effects of it, for I speak from experience when I say it has deprived us of several godly men who would have been ornaments to our Institution. **If such things are required to interest members of the Orange Institution - to act as a bond (as is alleged), all I can say is, it speaks but little for their genuine Protestantism. In my opinion the kind of Protestant that such and absurd profane farce pleases is the very sort we should be better without**" (19th January 1878).

George Kershaw, Orange Institution, England declared, "**I look upon all such innovations as the Black, the Blue, the Red, Green, White &c., as unworthy the acceptance of Protestants and the most certain way to bring the society down to the level of the Red Republican of 1793 or the Fenian Firebrand of 1865. I do not speak without reason, but can avouch all I have stated. I consider our Orange Fraternity as formed for the special protection of Protestantism as opposed to Paganism wherever found, whether in the form of babylonish rite and heathen mysteries of the followers of Nimrod, Bacchus, and Semiramis, or the Saturnalia of Pio Nono and the Whore of Rome, both having the same source and paternal derivation; but to take our stand on the Infallible Rock we contend earnestly for the faith once delivered to the saints, and as such we must root out from our midst this pollution, and have done with the chamber of imagery and witchcraft. Let us then put on the whole armour, standing shoulder to shoulder, for the truth.**

I am confident that the Purple Ritual has caused of our most eligible Protestant Churchmen to disconnect themselves from the fraternity. Wishing you God speed in this purging business " (26th January 1878).

post script

a challenge to christians within the Orange Institution of Ireland

There is little doubt from the evidence before us that there was a day when Orangeism strongly opposed the evil advances of the Royal Arch Purple Order. However, the same cannot be said today. The 20th Century has seen the gradual erosion of all opposition to this iniquitous degree.

In light of this change and the fact that the Orange Institution (whilst officially separate), is clearly the kindergarten for the Royal Arch Purple (95% of its members joining this order). Is it right for believers to remain within the Orange?

A searching soul within the Orange Institution may consider:

1. Can I be part of an order that is actively condoning sin?

2. Can I be part of an order that being a 'brotherhood' requires me to call a fellow member 'brother' irrespective of whether the member is a child of God or a child of the devil?

3. Is the compromise of the Orange Institution today, in its attitude to the Royal Arch Purple, symptomatic of an increasing fallen away within the Order which is openly revealed in its attitude to, and its condoning of, ecumenism (especially among the clergy)?

Psalms 1:1-3 declares, "**Blessed is the man that walketh not in the counsel of the ungodly, nor standeth in the way of sinners, nor sitteth in the seat of the scornful. But his delight is in the law of the LORD; and in his law doth he meditate day and night. And he shall be like a tree planted by the rivers of water, that bringeth forth his fruit in his season; his leaf also shall not wither; and whatsoever he doeth shall prosper**."